I AM YOUR SISTER: SEASON 2

I am Your Sister: Season 2

Ericka K. F. Simpson

Published by **EKS Books**
Macon, Georgia

This book is a work of fiction. Names, characters places, and incidents either are products of the author's imagination or are used fictitiously. Any resemblance to actual persons, living or dead, events or locales is entirely coincidental.

Unless otherwise indicated, all Scripture quotations are taken from the Holy Bible, New Living Translation, copyright © 1996, 2004, 2007 by Tyndale House Foundation. Used by permission of Tyndale House Publishers, Inc., Carol Stream, Illinois 60188. All rights reserved.

"*Children Need Positive Self-Concept*" excerpt written by Marian Frierson, quoted from Page 4 of The Perquimans Weekly, Hertford, NC, printed Thursday, January 31, 1991.

For information about booking author for an event or special discounts for bulk purchases, please contact Ericka K. F. Simpson at eksbooks@gmail.com.

Printed and published in the United States of America

ISBN-13: 9780615796918
ISBN-10: 0615796915

www.ekfsimpson.com
www.facebook.com/eksbooks
www.twitter.com/ekfsimpson

"I must write this novel, not only for others to read but to free *myself* of this sense of shame and fear." ~ from *Native Son* by Richard Wright

Present Day:

Memorial Day Weekend 2012

Pre-game Warm up

"THE LIFE OF A SUPERSTAR is poorer than the average person. The cries from the fans drown out the lies unfaithful lovers tell. The shine from the bling blinds us to the phoniness we willingly accept as friendship to fill the void of loneliness." ~ Symone Holmes, Lez Bian Magazine, Dec 2011.

Symone grimaced at the article the excited fan shoved in her chest. It was the first exclusive interview where she exposed more of her true self and the sight of it reminded her of that vulnerability. Within seconds though, she shrugged off the insecurities in letting her guard down and signed, *God Is Love – Sy*, across the top of the page.

Symone signed one last autograph before finally escaping the bottleneck tunnel filled with fans. She smiled at the thought of her new WNBA team, the Atlanta Dream, winning their home opener against the New York Liberty. The trade from Houston back in February caught her off guard but she was happy to be back on the east coast. The team had three more home games, which gave Symone another week to familiarize herself with the southern city better known as 'Hotlanta'. It was Friday night and with the game finally over, Memorial Day Weekend in Atlanta left her with limitless possibilities to celebrate her arrival.

Symone stood on the concrete sidewalk outside the player's entrance of the Philips Arena. She closed her eyes and inhaled a huge dose of humid Georgia air. *And I thought Texas was hot,* Symone thought as she hiked her gym bag up on her right shoulder. Symone took a few steps forward before opening her eyes. She nearly ran into a little girl wearing a replica of her basketball jersey.

"Oh shoot!" Symone said surprised as she braced herself from toppling over the fragile child by balancing on her toes.

The little girl barely blinked, her eyes dancing wildly at the sight of her favorite female basketball player.

"Hey," Symone said curiously, as she looked around for an adult. "Where you come from?"

The girl remained silent, her tiny fingers fiddling with the oversized numbers on the jersey.

"Kayleigh? Kayleigh?" A woman in her early thirties ran frantically to the little girl. "Oh, thank god!" She hugged Kayleigh then knelt down in front of her. "What did I tell you about walking away from me?"

Kayleigh glanced at the woman but quickly returned her gaze to Symone. The woman looked up at Symone and immediately recognized her.

Symone stared in awe at the face looking back at her. "Regina?"

Regina stood awkwardly to her feet, tugged at her denim jean leggings and grasped Kayleigh's hand in hers. She smiled and spoke softly, "Hi, Symone."

Symone was unsteady in her advance toward them. It had been close to seven years since she last saw Regina, more than five years since they last talked. Symone wanted to hug her but decided to let Regina initiate any physical contact, if any.

"Hey. Long time no see." Symone slid her hands deep into her jean pockets to hide her nerves. "I didn't know you were in town."

"My job transferred me to Atlanta back in January."

"January. Wow." Symone was surprised to hear that she and Regina lived in the same city for four months without contact.

"I thought about calling but—"

"No," Symone interrupted. "It's been a long time. I understand."

Symone smiled inwardly. Regina had aged gracefully. Thanks to the warm Georgia temperature, Regina's caramel complexion toasted to a deep golden brown. The A-line bob hairstyle cuffed her face at the chin and the maroon lipstick highlighted the fiery glow in her soft brown eyes.

"You are so beautiful," Symone said more to herself but still loud enough for Regina to hear.

Regina blushed. "Thank you." She avoided eye contact and used her free hand to fidget with her turquoise mesh tunic sweater that fell off her shoulder.

Symone noticed Regina rocked back on her heel, something she used to do when she felt uncomfortable.

"Sorry, I didn't mean—"

"It's okay," Regina said softly. "You um, you look good, too."

Symone smiled politely but she really wanted to kick herself. The unexpected meeting was awkward enough without her sounding like a dumbstruck teen still in love with an ex. Not to mention this was the first opportunity Symone had at impressing Regina and she was dressed like a high schooler in jeans and an *X-Men* T-shirt.

Why didn't I wear a nice pair of slacks and a decent shirt, Symone thought.

"These are just chill clothes," Symone said, trying to tuck in her shirttail inconspicuously. "Nothing like how you used to primp me back in the day."

"No, I guess not but you always liked your own style over mine."

"Yeah well, you know." Symone drew in a deep breath and exhaled slowly through her nose. Sweat poured from her pores as if she were back on the basketball court. She hoped breathing would bring her spiking temperature under control. The last thing she needed was for soil marks to develop under her armpits.

What is it about this woman that after all these years, she still has a hold over me?

Symone cleared her throat and turned her attention to young Kayleigh. "Did you have fun at the game?"

Kayleigh looked up at Regina as though she was waiting for permission to speak.

"It's okay, honey," Regina assured her.

Kayleigh just nodded.

"And your name is Kayleigh?"

Kayleigh nodded again.

Symone knelt down in front of her. "That's a beautiful name."

Kayleigh barely spoke above a whisper, "My mommy gave it to me."

Even though Symone assumed Kayleigh was Regina's daughter, hearing the word 'mommy' struck her harder than expected.

"Tell her how you're her biggest fan," Regina said.

Kayleigh clasped her hands together in front of her. She twisted her body back and forth, swinging her two ponytails and shielding her blushing smile. "I'm your biggest fan."

Symone quickly blinked back tears and replied, "Well, my biggest fan has to have my autograph, right?"

Kayleigh's eyes lit up as Symone pulled a black *Sharpie* pen out of her bag and signed Kayleigh's jersey.

"There." Symone leaned in and whispered, "Now you can get your mom to buy you another jersey so you can put this one in a frame on your wall."

Without warning, Kayleigh wrapped her tiny arms around Symone's neck. The smell of *Blue Magic* hair grease reminded Symone of her relaxer-free childhood days, consisting of hot combs, singed hair and burn marks on her forehead.

Emotions overwhelmed Symone as she welcomed Kayleigh's innocent, loving embrace. The steady flow of tears that fell down Symone's cheeks surprised Regina and brought tears to her own eyes. Regina knew Symone always wanted a family of her own. They talked about it constantly when they were a couple back in college. However, unfortunate events after Symone's graduation put them on a path neither one of them expected.

Part One

(7 years earlier)

Chapter 1

"God is our refuge and strength, always ready to
help in times of trouble." ~ Psalms 46:1

"IS MY TIE STRAIGHT?" Symone asked Regina.

Regina walked over and stood in front of
Symone. Tiny beads of sweat formed on Symone's
forehead and their cousins rolled happily down her back.

"Your tie is fine, baby," Regina smiled.

It was April 16th, the night of the 2005 WNBA
draft in Secaucus, New Jersey. Symone was predicted to
be the top pick in a draft class that included stellar college
players from Minnesota, Mississippi State, Houston, LSU
and Georgia.

Symone and Regina were in the green room
waiting for the draft to begin. The scene reminded her of
a beauty pageant, or how she thought a beauty pageant
would be; young women dressed in gowns and glittering
jewelry, mothers applying last minute makeup touchups
and fathers, boyfriends or significant others smiling
proudly at what the women had accomplished.

Danishes, iced and jelly-filled doughnuts and fruit
platters covered in watermelon, grapes, apples and
cantaloupe overflowed the long fold out table near the
back of the room. The sweet aroma of artificial and
natural sugars claimed a number of hungry souls but

Symone was too nervous to nibble on the finger food set out for the players and their families. Anxiety grew inside her as each passing minute ticked, putting her closer to a new life as a professional athlete.

Symone felt as though she was suffocating so she fiddled with her silk solid gray skinny tie anyway.

Regina popped her hand. "Now it's crooked," she said fixing it.

Regina smiled as she glanced over Symone's appearance. Symone's long, thick mane was freshly perm and fell just below her shoulder blades. Her slim frame had chiseled from four years of weight training during college. Symone only added eight pounds to her original weight of one hundred twelve pounds from her freshman year but she was proud to put on any weight at all. Regina convinced Symone not to wear a flashy suit and but begin her professional image with a classic executive style. The ash gray wool blend suit was tailored to fit Symone's slim physic like a glove. Paired with a raspberry with gray stripe shirt, people would definitely notice when Symone took center stage.

Symone drew in a long deep breath to calm her rapid heartbeat. "Everything has to be perfect. I'm making a statement here tonight, Reggie."

Regina loved the woman Symone had grown to be. The charming but mellow Symone gave way and allowed a more assertive yet sociable Symone to emerge. Even though she was still guarded with her emotions, Symone's evolution caused Regina to fall deeper in love with her than when they first met.

"You would've made a bigger statement if you wore a dress."

Symone looked at Regina with a raised eyebrow. "Now you know that's not me."

"I know," Regina smiled. "Still, you in a dress—"

"That would catch everybody off guard, wouldn't it?"

"We still have time if you want to do a quick switch-a-roo with me."

Symone stepped back and glanced at Regina's off the shoulder sweater dress. Regina wanted to match Symone's outfit without taking the spotlight off her so she kept her color choice simple in gray and black.

"I may have enough shape to fill the dress but those heels," Symone shook her head, "I see a major mishap in my future, most likely when the cameras are on me as I'm walking across the stage."

Regina held in her laugh as she brushed a piece of lint from Symone's lapel. "You're probably right. We better stay on the safe side and—"

"Symone Holmes," a man with a headset called into the green room, "you're needed on the main floor. We're about to begin."

IT SEEMED AS THOUGH another hour had passed before the selections actually began. Many of the potential first round draft players were doing pre-selection interviews while others waited nervously with family and friends.

Symone wiped her sweaty palms on her raspberry silk handkerchief as the President of the WNBA approached the podium.

"And with the first pick in the 2005 WNBA draft, the Charlotte Sting selects Symone Holmes from Marian University."

Symone smiled and hugged Regina before heading to the stage. She resisted the urge to adjust her tie again. Instead, she buttoned the two buttons on her suit jacket and stepped onto the stage. She grin a huge Kool-Aid smile as she walked toward President Orender. They shook hands and smiled as they each held a corner of the '05 Sting' jersey for the media to snap pictures.

After the photography session, a staff associate directed Symone to the back of the arena for a postselection interview session with sports reporter, Carrie Reynolds.

"Congratulations, Symone," Carrie greeted before the interview.

Symone shook her hand and took a seat in the cushioned armchair across from her. "Thanks."

Carrie looked toward the camera, flexed her facial muscles than straightened her posture. The cameraman gave her the 'okay' sign right before the red recording light turned on.

"We are here with the number one draft pick Symone Holmes. Symone, what has this day been like for you?"

"It's been crazy but that excited type of crazy. The day seemed to zoom by so quickly and then I get here and it seemed to come to a complete halt until my name was called. But, um," she cleared her throat, "I'm so happy to be here and I'm still soaking it all in."

"You'll be going to a team that's in a rebuilding season. What does it feel like knowing you're being brought in to help this franchise reach new heights in the league?"

Symone's phone vibrated indicating an incoming call. She inconspicuously pressed the IGNORE button and answered, "I'm actually looking forward to it. I think playing under Coach Lacey will be a great experience. She's a former player who studied the game under legendary coach, Kay Yow. I'm also blessed to play alongside veterans like Dawn Staley, Allison Feaster, Sheri Sam and Tangela Smith, all whom I've watched growing up and all whom have been an inspiration in me reaching this point in playing professional ball. I look forward to doing what I can to help us all reach that common goal in winning a championship for the city of Charlotte."

"You don't have long to think about the adjustment between college and the WNBA," Carrie said.

"You start training camp in a few weeks. What is it like going from college to pro in such a short period of time?"

Symone smiled and replied, "Well, I haven't got a taste of the pros yet but it will definitely be a quick transition. I have final exams coming up so now I have to revert to college life and graduate. But I think it's an advantage because I'm already in basketball shape. I know the league will be more physical," playfully flexed her muscles to the camera, "so I tried to bulk up a bit. But I'm ready to show what I have to offer to the league."

Carrie paused as the second draft pick was announced. Symone shifted in her seat as her phone vibrated again. She grabbed at her side and quickly silenced it.

"Okay Symone," Carrie started back up, "I have just one more question for you. What are you looking forward to the most in playing in the WNBA?"

Symone thought for a moment then responded, "Playing with the veteran talent in the league and putting my stamp on history by being a part of the WNBA organization." Symone reached down and silenced the vibration for a third time. "I look forward to carrying and passing the torch to the next group of women basketball players when it's all said and done."

"Thank you for your time Symone and good luck this season and on your WNBA career."

"Thanks Carrie."

Symone stepped off the stage and immediately checked her phone. There were missed calls from her coaches and a few of her teammates but there was one number she didn't expect to see; a '757' area code she hadn't seen in a long time.

Regina noticed the bewildered look on Symone's face. "You okay?" she asked.

"My dad called," Symone said surprised.

"What did he say?"

"I don't know. He called during the interview so I missed it."

"Did he leave a message?" Regina asked.

Symone searched through her voicemail log and saw that her dad did leave a message. She walked to the back of the green room and sat down.

It had been almost six months since Symone last talked to her father. His birthday was in January and after receiving her birthday card in the mail, he called.

"Heyyy."

"Hey Dad. How you doing?"

"Not too bad. How 'bout you?"

"I'm good. On my way to practice."

"I'm not gonna hold you up then. I finally got around to opening the mail and I saw your card. Just wanted to call and say thank you."

"It's not everyday you turn sixty, you know."

"Like the old saying goes, 'sixty puts you halfway to heaven'."

Symone smiled because the only person she ever heard say that saying was her father.

"Did you do anything special?" Symone asked.

"Not yet. Me and James going down to the races in Daytona next month."

"Oh okay. That's cool."

"Well, I'll let you go. Just wanted to say thank you for the card."

"You're welcome, dad."

"Be safe and I'm still praying for you."

"You too, dad."

"Love you."

"Love you, too."

Symone shook her head quickly to snap herself back to the present. After letting out a slow deep breath, she put the phone to her ear and listened to the waiting voice message.

Heyyy Symone, it's your father. I'm guessing you busy with school or playing ball but I was calling to let you know your mom is in the hospital. She had a stroke...

She closed her eyes to steady the spinning of the room. Her heart pounded so hard her chest hurt. The rest of the message became faint muffled sounds in Symone's ear. She sat the phone on the table next to her and wrung her hands to stop them from shaking. Tears formed in her eyes every time her father's voice paused and gave way to sniffled and cracked speech as he forced the rest of the bad news out. Symone finally hit the end button unable to listen to another word. She sat back in the chair, her posture slumped and worn.

"Baby, what's wrong?" Regina asked.

"I—I think I gotta go home," Symone said calmly, her eyes filled with tears.

"What happened?"

"My mom had a stroke." The statement flowed from her lips effortlessly but she wasn't surprised at how poised she was. Remaining calm during traumatic times was one of her strongest qualities. What Symone was unsure about was how she would react when staring that tragedy square in the face.

"Oh my god!" Regina gasped. She wrapped her arms around Symone's neck and kissed her softly on the cheek. "I'm so sorry," she whispered in her ear.

Regina felt the wetness from Symone's tears as they landed on her bare shoulders.

Symone raised her head and wiped her face with the palms of her hands. "I gotta go home," she repeated. "I gotta go home."

"Of course." Regina pulled out her phone and called 411 to get the number to the airport.

Symone sat in a daze as Regina retrieved the information and called the airport to make flight arrangements.

"Yes, two tickets to Norfolk International in Virginia," Regina spoke into the phone.

"No," Symone stated quickly.

"Hold on one moment," Regina said to the reservationist. "What was that?" she asked Symone.

"Just one ticket, Reggie."

"Symone—"

"Please don't fight me on this. I gotta do this alone."

Regina let out a saddened sigh. "Ma'am," she returned to the reservationist on the line, "Make that one ticket to Norfolk. The first flight you have available."

Chapter 2

DEAFENING SILENCE ENGULFED THE drive to the airport. Symone stared out the window to avoid Regina's disappointing eyes cutting in her direction every few minutes.

"It just isn't the right time, Reggie."

"It's never the right time," Regina said in a biting tone.

Symone turned her head toward Regina but stared at the stick shift console. "My mother's in the hospital," she raised her eyes slightly, "I can't just—throw this on her. It'd be too much."

"Baby, we can't keep hiding from her."

Symone loosened her tie and unbuttoned the top button on her shirt. "We're not hiding. She *knows* about us. Both my parents do."

"But you're feeding her denial by avoiding the situation. We're hiding in plain sight and you know it."

Regina parked the car in the drop off area in front of the airport.

"Give me a chance to get down there first to see how she's doing at least." Symone sighed. She motioned to open the door then paused. "I haven't talked to her in four years, Reggie. I just need to make sure she's okay."

Regina remained in the car while Symone checked in at the outside counter. It wasn't the time to bring up Symone's damaged relationship with her mother or how it needed to be fixed. Tonight was supposed to be a celebratory night for the two of them. Unfortunately, their happiness would be delayed a little longer than planned.

Regina set her reservations aside and finally exited the car. Symone stood on the curb with her carry-on bag in her hand.

"Go be with your family," Regina said in an easy tone. "Your mind's not going to rest until you know she's okay."

The tension in Symone's shoulders quickly dissipated like air escaping from a balloon. "Thanks baby. When you heading back to Charlotte?"

"Tomorrow afternoon. I'll call you when I get there."

Symone leaned forward and gave Regina a soft but quick peck on the lips. "I love you," she mouthed as she disappeared into the airport.

Symone wasn't expecting the trip to be long so she only packed her carry-on. The stares she received as she walked through the terminal made her wish she had changed into something more casual. She was sure not too many people in New Jersey were used to seeing a woman dressed in a men's suit in public. Symone pretended to ignore the confused looks as she found a seat tucked away in the corner behind the flight desk to rest. Her phone still buzzed with calls and texts from people congratulating her on her impending success but she couldn't muster the will to respond. Not knowing the outcome of the night's events dragged her soul to a place it never liked to swim, worry-infested waters.

Symone had an hour wait before her flight boarded. She started to close her eyes and zone out of reality when she felt a pair on her. The soft features smiled when acknowledged. Symone nodded casually to the woman dressed in military fatigues sitting across from her. Symone didn't realize it back then but basketball conditioning was a lot like military training and she was sure it would be just as gruesome in the WNBA. Symone witnessed basic military training firsthand the summer before her sophomore year of high school when her summer league team played in a tournament sponsored by the Air Force. That was the summer Symone's life changed drastically, with basketball and with her family.

****

Symone was so excited she could hardly sleep. Her AAU summer league basketball team, the Hampton Roads Jaguars, was in San Antonio, Texas playing in the championship game against the Sacramento Basin of California in the Lackland Youth Classic. The coach brought the team down for the six-week summer camp hosted by the Air Force base prior to the tournament just so the team could get a closer look at the west coast style of play. Both teams were undefeated in their brackets and it was time to see what region of the country reigned supreme in 16-17 year girls basketball.

As always, Symone was the first from her team to leave the barracks. She liked the idea of staying on a military installation instead of at one of the downtown hotels. Team sport activities resembled war, the opposing team were the enemy and the championship title was the spoils of winning the battle. Waking to reveille every morning put Symone in the mindset of a warrior. She believed the sights of the battle dress uniforms, fatigues, and the sound of the boots pounding the pavement provided her team the emotional lift they needed to play their best game and come away victorious.

Symone cuffed her basketball under her arm and smiled a cocky grin at the basic trainees suffering through morning physical training. Symone watched as a Military Instructor lied down next to a scrawny boy with glasses that reminded her of a windshield on a 1942 Studebaker Champion, a vehicle she was very familiar with thanks to her father's love in restoring old cars. The instructor yelled at the boy as he struggled to complete the correct form for standard pushups receptively. The instructor was so close, sweat dripped from the boy's brow and landed on the brim of the instructor's hat. The instructor's face turned fiery red and Symone anticipated smoke was about to shoot out his ears just as it did on Saturday morning cartoons. The instructor jumped to his feet and demanded more pushups as punishment for the perspiration unintentionally intruding on his person.

Symone's jaw tightened. "That couldn't be me," she said aloud. Smiling at the basketball, she corrected, "Not for nothing but the game."

The sun gleamed bright as Symone began a light jog on the running trail. The main lodging facility was 1.4 miles away, a good distance to loosen up the muscles first thing in the morning before a physically demanding day. Her Jaguars warm-up jacket pasted to her skin because of the increased heat index but she refused to take it off. Coach advised the team college scouts were attending the championship game and if any were staying on base, Symone wanted them to take a personal notice of her work ethic.

"Morning, Symone."

The front desk clerk's sweet Spanish tone instantly brought a smile to Symone's face.

"Hi, Rosa. Any mail for me?" It had been a few days and she was looking forward to hearing from Kidera again. Reading how much she missed her made Symone smile.

"Ah, ah, ah."

Upon the team's arrival, Symone made the mistake in revealing to Rosa that she wanted to learn Spanish. The comment was an innocent attempt at flirting but it gave Rosa the opportunity to share her heritage.

Symone tossed the basketball back and forth as she thought. "Um, ¿Cualquier correo para mí?" she spoke slowly.

Rosa smiled. "Your 'friend' would be proud."

Symone blushed as Rosa checked the bin. Was it that obvious their conversations over the past few weeks disclosed she had a girlfriend?

"Just one letter, mamí," Rosa said.

Symone looked at the letter surprised. It was not from Kidera but from her brother, Antoine. She waved goodbye to Rosa and opened the letter as she walked out the door. Symone came to a complete halt and tried to steady her shaking hands as they clutched the paper.

Sy,
Mom and Dad been tripping the last few days. I don't know what happened but they called me. I guess they decided to clean your room. They found some books about GAYS and stuff. They also got a book that you write in. Mom read it and was crying. They asking me questions but I'm playing the slow role. I've been away at college for a year now so it's easy for me to get away with saying, 'I don't know'.
Things aren't going to be the same when you get back. They talking 'bout bringing back family prayer and they asking me too many questions. Mom feels like she didn't do a good job of raising you or she did something wrong. I'm letting you know so you can be prepared for it. Wish I could be there to help you through it but coach got us swamped with summer league camps this summer. Holla at me if you need me. You know I always got your back.

Love ya baby
sis,
Antoine

The ground shifted beneath her as though an earthquake had hit. Nausea swooped in unannounced and Symone had to swallow hard to keep it from taking flight. "Keep it together, Sy," she whispered to herself. Passing out was not an option. Any sign of weakness would alert the enemy and cost her team a championship title. Symone's eyes darted from one end of the street to the other in search of opposing players on the prowl. Her heart raced as she stuffed the letter in her jacket pocket. This can't be happening, not now, she thought. This was supposed to be the best day of her life but it just turned into the worst. Her parents now knew she was gay and they were currently on a plane on their way to see her. "There was no way they would bring it up, not today," Symone tried to convince herself as she stammered back to the barracks.

****

"NOW BOARDING FIRST CLASS and persons with disabilities on flight 2837 to Norfolk, Virginia," the announcer said across the PA system.

Symone grabbed her carry-on bag from the seat next to her and headed to the boarding line. A young girl with scraggly blonde hair and bright green eyes watched carefully as Symone stood in line behind her. Symone was not sure if the little girl holding her mother's hand was staring at her because she had on a suit or because she was a basketball fan. Symone forced a smile then reached into her bag and pulled out an autographed miniature basketball. The little girl's eyes grew wide in delight, which made Symone's heart warm in pleasure. Symone held out the ball and the little girl took it out of her hand gingerly. The little girl turned around and held the gift up for her mother to see. The mother peered over her shoulder and eyed Symone suspiciously. The mother bent over, whispered something in the little girl's ear then held her firmly by her shoulders directly in front of her.

Under normal circumstances, Symone would have responded to the gesture with a 'nice nasty' remark especially since neither of them said thank you for the gift. However, Symone had to save her energy to fight the ignorance that lingered within her own family.

****

"THAT WAS A GREAT game you played out there," Symone's dad said.

Symone's summer league basketball team won the championship game and she received Most Valuable Player award of the tournament. Most high school players would have been ecstatic after a game like that especially when the college recruits looked thoroughly impressed. However, Symone sat across the table from her parents, sweat pouring from her pores like bullets fired from an automatic weapon.

"Thanks dad," Symone replied, her eyes buried in her plate of chicken enchiladas and refried beans.

"You'll probably get to pick whatever college you want to go to."

"Yeah, probably."

"Have you thought about it?"

Symone finally looked up at her dad. His eyes were calm and comforting. Not what Symone expected from a man who just found out his daughter was gay.

"A little," Symone replied. She felt relaxed in her father's gaze. "I wanna go to North Carolina but it's a big school. I'm not used to being in class with a hundred other students."

Her dad smiled. "That's my girl. Thinking about school, not just about the game."

"I still have time though. I'm only gonna be a sophomore and coaches can't contact me 'til my junior year."

"That's right but this exposure is a great start to the upcoming year."

"Yeah," Symone said with a lopsided grin. "Coach said the same thing. He said colleges will definitely be keeping an eye on me after the way I played today."

"He's right."

The ease of the conversation gave Symone the confidence to look in her mother's direction. The torched stare she delivered burned Symone's eyes so bad, tears formed instantly.

"Well, I better go make a pit stop before we head out," her dad grunted as he belched and left the table.

Symone opened her mouth to plead for him to wait but no words followed through in the task.

As soon as her dad wrapped the corner to the men's room, Symone's mother unloaded on her.

"Do you have something to tell me?" Before Symone could answer, her mother carried on, "Why do you think you're a..." She paused unable to say the word 'lesbian'. "Why do you think you're that way? Who told you? Where did you even learn about it?"

Symone didn't answer right away. She wasn't sure if her mother was finished bombarding her with questions, all of which she had no answers to.

"I don't know," Symone finally spoke up. "I just do. I think I've always liked girls. I just didn't know until—"

"No," her mother cut her off. "I didn't teach you about that. You didn't learn that kind of behavior in my house."

"It's not something you learn, ma."

"You had to get it from somewhere. I know you didn't just wake up feeling like this. All that reading you do, those books we found—"

"Yeah, reading made me gay," Symone grunted under her breath.

"Don't you dare talk to me like that young lady. And you will not claim this—this sin. Not—"

Symone's father appearing from around the corner robbed her mother of her final statement.

"So, have you thought about what other schools you might want to go to if UNC's not the one?" he asked as he sat back down at the table.

Symone watched as her mother at her food in silence. Her passivity was unusual and caught Symone off guard. She could've sworn Antoine's letter said 'Mom and Dad' but maybe he was wrong. Her mother wouldn't keep something of this magnitude from him, would she? And if so, why?

"Um, not really."

Symone paid attention to every detail of her father's demeanor. His posture was open and inviting. His mustache and beard framed his smile like a fine portrait hanging on the wall. Signs of wrinkles mysteriously eluded his milk chocolate skin, affording him the pleasure of looking ten years younger than the forty-four years he's credited with living.

"Well, you have time," her dad said smiling at her. "Keep this up and we'll have a few campuses to visit in the near future to help you decide."

****

SYMONE RESTED IN THE first class seat as best she could. The images from her high school days swarmed her mind like bees to a honey jar. The only thing she knew could bring her relief was the Word so she reached into her carry-on bag and pulled out her Bible. She turned to her favorite passage, Psalms 91.

Symone was very familiar with the passage, especially the New Living Translation. She tried reading it to herself but the sound of the flight attendant explaining and demonstrating safety instructions broke her concentration. Symone grabbed the headphones used to listen to music or watch in-flight movies from the seat pocket in front of her. She placed them over her ears to muffle the flight attendant's voice and tried reading to herself again. Still unable to meditate fully on the passage, Symone began reading aloud to herself.

1 Those who live in the shelter of the Most High will find rest in the shadow of the Almighty. 2

*This I declare about the Lord: He alone is my
refuge, my place of safety; he is my God, and I
trust him. 3 For he will rescue you from every
trap and protect you from deadly disease. 4 He
will cover you with his feathers. He will shelter
you with his wings. His faithful promises are your
armor and protection. 5 Do not be afraid of the
terrors of the night, nor the arrow that flies in the
day. 6 Do not dread the disease that stalks in
darkness, nor the disaster that strikes at midday.
7 Though a thousand fall at your side, though ten
thousand are dying around you, these evils will not
touch you.*

Symone nodded and smiled inwardly as the
affirmation of God's word settled the toiling in her soul.

*8 Just open your eyes, and see how the wicked are
punished. 9 If you make the Lord your refuge, if
you make the Most High your shelter, 10 no evil
will conquer you; no plague will come near your
home. 11 For he will order his angels to protect
you wherever you go. 12 They will hold you up
with their hands so you won't even hurt your foot
on a stone. 13 You will trample upon lions and
cobras; you will crush fierce lions and serpents
under your feet! 14 The Lord says, "I will rescue
those who love me. I will protect those who trust in
my name. 15 When they call on me, I will
answer; I will be with them in trouble. I will
rescue and honor them. 16 I will reward them
with a long life and give them my salvation."*

As Symone finished reading, she felt someone
watching her. She glanced out the corner of her eye and
found the elderly woman sitting next to her staring at her.

Symone slowly turned her head and made eye contact with the blue eyes focused intently in her direction.

The crows feet in the corner of the woman's eyes mimicked marionette strings as they curled upward and brought a smile to the woman's face.

"God is always the answer, isn't he?" She spoke in a warm and soothing tone, the way hot cocoa relaxed your body on a cold winter night.

"Yes he is," Symone smiled. "Yes he is."

The woman placed her clammy, wrinkled hand on top of Symone's and said, "Whatever you're going through, you have to trust he'll make everything all right."

"I do," Symone said, somewhat guarded. She enjoyed indulging in spiritual conversations but she usually steered clear of them with strangers to avoid having to defend how her Christianity and sexuality could coexist.

The woman returned her hand to her side of the armrest and braced herself for the takeoff. She closed her eyes and hummed as the plane settled in the air.

"The greatest deceit the devil uses to get us out of the will of God is convincing us God is not true to his word." Symone looked over at the woman, her eyes closed. She continued speaking as if to no one in particular, "When we take matters into our own hands, we are saying we doubt God will take care of it for us. Where there's doubt, fear is not far behind and it's in that fear, the devil resides."

Chapter 3

"Even when I walk through the darkest valley, I will not be afraid, for you are close beside me."
~ Psalms 23:4

SYMONE RUSHED INTO THE emergency room without stopping at the sign in desk. She tried to gain access to the intensive care unit but the double doors would not open.

"Ma'am?"

Symone ignored the receptionist. She scanned the walls and saw the handicap access button. Symone hit the button and the doors slowly began to open.

"Ma'am!"

Symone combed the halls of the intensive care unit with the receptionist fast on his heels. She stopped when she saw her brother sitting outside a blue curtained room. "Antoine—"

He stood up and they held each other in a tight embrace.

The receptionist decided against interrupting them to verbally accost Symone. She frowned before heading back to her station.

"How she doing?" Symone asked Antoine.

She noticed his eyes were red but there was no sign of tears.

"The right side of her body's paralyzed."

What happened?"

Antoine sat back down and slumped in the chair. "Dad said he came home from work and took a shower. When he got out, he found her on the floor."

"Do they know what happened, what caused it?"

"He trying to get answers now," Antoine said, pointing at their father talking with a doctor.

Symone hoped her dad was in the room with her mom. It had been close to four years since she and her mother talked or seen each other and Symone was not sure of the reaction. She thought about waiting for her dad but decided against it.

Symone peeped her head around the curtain like a child sneaking a peek at a naked woman. "I can do all things through Christ which strengthens me. I can do all things through Christ which strengthen me," Symone repeated silently under her breath. Even now, Symone knew she needed more than her own will to face her mother.

Symone saw that her mother's eyes were closed and slowly moved to the foot of the hospital bed. She quickly removed her tie and stuffed it into her pants pocket. She slid her hands down the sides of her suit jacket to dry her sweaty palms.

Symone stared at the right side of her mother's face and immediately noticed the slight drooping. Bells sounded off in her ears, alerting her to the severity of her mother's condition. Symone's automatic response was to attack the threat with prayer so she closed her eyes and spoke to God silently.

The intensity of her words caused Symone to grip the rails of the hospital bed so tight it produced a popping sound that woke her mother.

Paula blinked a few times before setting her gaze on Symone. Her eyes narrowed in obvious disapproval.

"Hey ma," Symone said in a whisper. She was afraid the emotions of seeing her mother in such a vulnerable state would cause her voice to crack if she spoke louder.

Paula didn't respond. She continued to stare at Symone with her face twisted in a scowl.

Symone tried to ignore the hard glare. She cleared her throat and said, "I came as soon as I got dad's message." Paula's eyes never left Symone as she moved to the side of the hospital bed. "I'm glad you're okay." Symone smiled weakly but it still sparked no response from her mother. "I know you're probably tired so I'll let you rest." Symone leaned in to kiss her mother on the cheek but Paula turned her head away.

The purposeful negative reaction caught Symone off guard but the single word that escaped Paula's lips caused Symone's heart to drop down into the pit of her stomach.

Symone didn't know whether Paula said 'go' or 'no' but both demands delivered the same message. Her mother did not want her there.

Symone stepped outside the blue curtain and pulled it closed behind her. She sat down next to Antoine, closed her eyes and laid her head back against the wall.

"How was the draft?" Antoine asked out of nowhere.

"It was cool," Symone said not moving from her resting position.

"I meant to try and make it but—"

"It's cool," Symone cut him off. "You had more important things to take care of. I get it."

"Whoa—" Antoine said annoyed. "You know it's not even like that."

Symone leaned forward and looked Antoine square in the eyes. "You know what I know, Ant? I know

I should be out celebrating being drafted number one into the WNBA. I should have Regina by my side, you, dad *and* mom but I wasn't gonna get that and I was cool with it." Symone sniffed and wiped the tears that began to fall from her eyes. "Then dad calls me while I'm being interviewed and some part of me actually thought he was calling to congratulate me, but no. His message said he thought I was out playing ball or busy doing schoolwork. *He* didn't even know. And with all that, I *still* jumped on a plane, no hesitation, to come and check on a mother who doesn't even want me here."

Symone stood to her feet abruptly. Antoine grabbed her by the arm to keep her from walking away from him.

"Did she say something to you?"

"She don't ever say nothing to me, Ant. She just—stares like—" she sighed sadly, "I'm no good." Symone stared past him with a solemn look on her face. "I don't know why I thought this time would be any different."

"So, what, you just gonna leave?"

Antoine's defiant tone surprised Symone but she refused to waiver from her decision.

"Why stay?" Symone held her arms out to her sides and moved toward the exit. "She don't want me here."

Symone bumped into her father who just finished talking to the doctor.

"Symone?"

"Hey dad."

Frederick wrapped his arms around her. "I see you got my message."

"Yeah."

"Dad," Antoine stepped closer to them, "you need to talk some sense into her."

"Me?"

Frederick stood confused as Antoine and Symone continued to argue in the hallway.

"Yes you. Acting like her isn't going to fix—"

"I shouldn't be the one trying to fix anything. She cut me off!"

"Shh!" the nurse behind the desk hushed at them irritably.

Antoine took Symone by the arm and moved her to the corner of the hall. "It doesn't matter. God doesn't judge us on how other people treat us. It's all about how we treat them."

"I came, I expressed my concern and she told me to leave."

Frederick stepped in. "She just had a stroke, Symone. She doesn't know—"

"No dad, she knows. She knows."

"You're never going to feel at home until you square this," Antoine stated plainly.

Through a sorrowful half grin, Symone replied, "I'm going back to Charlotte. That's my home now."

Chapter 4

"Instead, let the Spirit renew your thoughts
and attitudes." ~ Ephesians 4:23

WATERSIDE FESTIVAL MARKETPLACE WAS alive
late Saturday night. Symone knew the favorite restaurant
spots, Joe's Crab Shack and Freemason Abbey were
packed to the brim. By the time on the car dashboard
which read 12:47am, she assumed BAR nightclub was
almost filled to capacity as well. Symone drove up and
down several blocks and was unable to find a parking
spot on the street. As much as she hated to pay the ten
dollars, she finally settled for using the public parking
garage.

The night air was cool so Symone decided to keep
her suit jacket on as she exited the garage and stepped
onto the street corner. Groups of people and happy
couples passed her on their way to a fun night on the
town. They seemed to move at a fast forward pace but
Symone was stuck in pause. She slowly weaved her way
through the crowd and found an empty bench in front of
the boat dock. Symone slumped down onto the bench
and used her palms to shield her face.

"This is supposed to be the best day of my life!" she shouted into her hands. "Why the devil's always gotta be messing up *my* day?"

Symone closed her eyes and took a minute to settle herself. She thought about the last time she sat at the boat dock at Waterside and realized she griped about the same thing back then. It seemed every year she was sitting before the water looking for answers to the same question.

Symone studied the Waterside setting and noticed how much the area had grown. Downtown Norfolk was turning into a huge tourist attraction with Nautilus, the maritime museum and science center and the new MacAuthur Center Mall. The biggest attraction was the HRT Ferry. Locals and tourists could take a sightseeing cruise across the Elizabeth River or take a short ferry ride to Downtown Portsmouth to the check out the Children's museum or the Sports Hall of Fame. Symone wanted to be proud of her hometown's growth but it was hard to do when she still felt her growth was stunted.

"Everything around me is changing, Lord. Progressing to—bigger, better things but me—I'm just—stagnate."

Symone slouched on the bench and hung her head in sadness. No matter how much she tried to move on, she always seemed to find herself facing the same unresolved issues year after year. Even when life seemed good, her relationship with Regina and living out her dream of playing in the WNBA, Symone could not escape the need for acceptance and love from those who were supposed to matter most, her blood. The look on her mother's face tonight reminded her of how long she had been fighting this losing battle.

****

SYMONE LAY IN HER bed staring at the ceiling. She had been home a week and her mother had not spoken to her since the interrogation after the summer camp basketball tournament in Texas. Luckily, Symone had been busy with calligraphy orders, which gave her a reason not to come home during the day. Symone caught on early that her mother did not talk about her disapproval of her being gay in her father's presence. She was not sure why but whatever the reason, Symone played on it to the best of her ability by staying away from the house until her father was home from work. Unfortunately, he was running late one day and that left Symone unprotected and vulnerable.

"You still never said why you think you're that way," Paula stated sourly. A frown creased her brow as she stood with her arms folded across her chest in the doorway of Symone's bedroom.

Symone sat up and turned to face her mother. "I, I don't know. I just don't look at boys that way."

"How do you know? You've never dated one."

"'Cause I'm not interested in dating one."

"You think I raised you to be like this?" Paula poked herself with her pointer finger. "What about your grandma, huh? You think she would approve of this?"

"I—"

"She had as much to do with raising you as I did. You think she would like you being this way?"

"I—I really don't know," Symone answered, her eyes staring sheepishly at the unleveled brown carpet.

"You're too smart for this, Symone." Paula shook her head. "The world doesn't like people like that."

"I don't care about what the world thinks, ma. I just need for you and dad—"

"You're not getting my blessing on this," Paula said as if the very idea was preposterous. "I will not accept it."

"So what are you saying? You're not accepting me? Your daughter?"

Paula squared her shoulders, placed her hands on her hips and stated firmly, "You are NOT my daughter. I didn't raise you to be like this. I'm ashamed of who you are and I want no part of it. None!"

******

THE VIBRATION FROM SYMONE'S phone temporarily interrupted her flashback. She looked at the caller ID and saw it was her brother. She ignored the call without a second thought. Moments later, a text message came through.

Antoine: *Just wanna ck where u sleeping*

Symone just realized she had not thought about her sleeping arrangements. She was so focused on her mother's well-being and that of her own hurt feelings that she never made plans on where to sleep. She thought about calling Kyra but quickly dispelled the thought from her head. Their friendship never recovered from Kyra hiding the fact that Symone's ex-girlfriend, Kidera had cheated on her. Symone understood that Kyra and Kidera were sisters but she still felt betrayed by her *then* best friend. At that moment, Symone would have given anything to have both of them back in her life. Kyra and Kidera were there for her when things were bad with her mother. Most importantly, their family accepted Symone and welcomed her warmly when her family disowned her. Now Symone felt as though she had no one to lean on or turn to except God and even He appeared to be missing in action at that moment.

Symone decided the best thing to do was to stay at a hotel. Antoine had a spare room but she was not ready to have him give her another ear full on being the bigger person. Staying at her father's house was definitely out of the question. She made up her mind and texted Antoine her answer.

Symone: *crashing at hotel. call u 2morro*

The mental jackhammer surrounding Symone's life drilled her temples steadily so she headed back to the parking garage to retrieve the rented Corolla. She sat in the car for a few moments and debated on what her next move should be. She was hungry but eating right before going to sleep would only give her heartburn. She could eat something light then drive around to tour the progress of the city but she was too tired. It was late but she knew her dad would still be at the hospital by her mother's side. Even though they were divorced, her dad never stopped loving the mother of his two children. He would sleep in the chair next to her bed until she came home if the doctors let him. Symone knew the house would be empty and she was interested to see what changes he had made but tonight would be too soon. Her mind was already flooded with emotion and walking through those doors may overwhelm her to the point of a breakdown. The only option left was to go to bed hungry.

"Nothing's working in my favor tonight, boy I tell you," Symone said as she started the car and drove to the nearest hotel to rest.

Chapter 5

"I will praise the LORD at all times. I will
constantly speak his praises." ~ Psalms 34:1

EVEN WITHOUT AN ALARM, Symone still found
herself waking up at 6am. Preseason basketball
conditioning always trained her body's self-clock and it
usually did not shut itself off until a few weeks before
summer. Symone thought the stress of the previous
night's events would force her to sleep a few hours longer
but luck would not provide her that luxury either.

Symone reached over and glanced at her phone's
home screen. She placed her phone on silent before going
to bed. She texted Regina to let her know she made it to
Virginia safely but other than that, Symone was not in the
mood to talk to anyone.

Her phone showed a few missed calls from her
dad, her brother and her agent. Symone rolled onto her
back and sighed as she stared at the ceiling. Thoughts of
defeat flooded her mind but she refused to give them life
by speaking them aloud. Instead, Symone recited, "I win.
I am the righteousness of God by faith and I win." Tears
weld in Symone's eyes as she repeated it over and over
again.

After ten minutes of spiritual meditation, Symone
finally smiled and sat up on the bed. She threw her legs
over the side and grabbed her bible from her bag. She

looked down at the floor and replied with a wink, "It don't matter how hard you come at me, devil. The fight is rigged. I've already won."

Symone read the *Our Daily Bread* devotional for the morning and prayed before returning phone calls. The first call made was to her agent. Symone knew the only thing he needed to know was when she was coming back to Charlotte so he could set up a meeting with The Sting organization to discuss contract terms.

The next call she made was to her father.

"Hello?"

Symone smiled. Her dad was still an early riser even after retiring from the shipyard three years ago. His voice sounded as though he had been up for a while.

"Hey dad."

"Well hi there Ms. Symone."

"I meant to call you once I got settled in last night but I hit the bed and it was lights out."

Frederick chuckled half-heartedly. "I figured you were beat with being up all day then traveling here."

"Yeah, I guess I didn't know how tired I was until I laid down." Symone looked down at herself and saw she still had on her suit. "I didn't even change. Just slept in my clothes."

There was a brief silence and Symone knew the apology was coming. She temporarily delayed the inevitable and asked, "So, do they know what caused the stroke?"

The rustling from her dad rubbing his hand against his stubby beard echoed through the phone. "She stopped taking her blood pressure medication."

"Blood pressure medication?" Symone said surprised.

"Yep. Both me and your mom take blood pressure medicine."

Symone never knew either one of her parents had health issues or why her mother would put hers more in jeopardy. "So, why she do that?"

"I don't think it was intentional. Sometimes she forgets and skips a day—"

"How do you—never mind." Symone bit her tongue to avoid judging her mother's action verbally to her dad. "She's gonna be fine though, right?"

"She's going to need physical therapy but the doctors say it's nothing she can't recover from."

"Well, that's good." Symone sighed in relief. "I'm glad she's gonna be okay."

"Symone, your mom, she didn't mean—"

"Dad don't," Symone cut him off. She let out a deep breath to remain calm. "Don't apologize for her. I mean, It is what it is."

"She still need some time to get used to it, is all."

"Y'all've known since right before my sophomore year of high school and I'm graduating college, dad. Time is *not* the issue."

"Well, I'm still praying she'll come around. I hope you're still praying too."

Through a deep sigh, Symone replied, "Yeah, I'm still praying. Look um, I have a few more calls to return. I just wanted to call you back and let you know I'm heading back to North Carolina later today." Before he could respond, Symone continued, "I have to meet with the team and get ready for the season."

Frederick paused but replied, "All right then. Have you talked to your brother?"

"Not yet. I was gonna call him next."

"I won't hold you up then. I'm still praying for you and I love you."

"Love you too, dad."

After hanging up with her father, Symone started to call Antoine but decided against it. She knew the conversation would be the same as the one she had with her father and she was not in the mood to hear it again. She needed strength in the form of a good breakfast first. Besides, it was still early and he had kids. He needed all the sleep he could get so she texted him instead.

Symone: *leaving for NC today but hitting up Fairlawn about noon b4 I go*

Symone waited a few minutes for a return text. When there was no immediate response, she decided to call Regina.

"Hmm?"

"Wow," Symone smiled at Regina's greeting. "There must be some serious morning breath behind those lips."

"Hush," Regina grumbled into the phone. "What time is it?"

"Almost seven."

"I really need your body's time clock to do better."

"Nope so you better start getting used to it especially since I'm gonna be around more."

"Yes, I know." Regina yawned then asked, "How's your mom doing?"

Symone heard a beep. She looked down at her phone and saw that Antoine had replied to her text.

Antoine: *you going to 8am service?*

"Shoot, I forgot today was Sunday," Symone said aloud.

"What?" Regina said confused.

"My bad, Reggie. Antoine texted me about church and I didn't realize today was Sunday. Hold on a second okay?"

Symone: *Forgot today was Sunday so no. Get me a CD*

"Okay, I'm back," Symone said. "She's fine, fine enough to still not want me around."

"I'm sorry, baby."

"It's cool. I'm coming back today," Symone politely changed the subject.

"Already?"

"Yeah well, there's no need for me to stay longer."

Another beep interrupted their conversation.

Antoine: *Cool. Will meet you at the courts*

"I'm driving back though," Symone said after reading Antoine's text. "Planning on stopping to see my Aunt in Elizabeth City and visit my grandma."

"Okay. Just call me before you get on the road."

"I will. I'm gonna go find something to eat so you go 'head and go back to sleep."

"I love you, Symone."

"I love you too, Reggie."

SYMONE SAT ON THE hood of the rental car and twirled the basketball in her hands. There were a few vacant courts and Symone stared at them as if she were trying to determine which one would become her first victim.

"Number one draft pick and you rent a Toyota Corolla?"

Symone playfully punched her brother as he walked up beside her.

"Now you know WNBA players don't get paid like you big time NBA stars."

Antoine was the first in the family to become a professional athlete, playing six years with the Philadelphia 76ers before tearing his ACL in his right knee for the second time last season. Instead of rehabbing and trying to make another comeback, Antoine retired. He felt this was his opportunity to take time off and pursue his second passion, music. The money he earned as a professional basketball player was invested well by his wife Nicole so there was nothing holding him back from stepping out on this new venture.

"You don't need it." Antoine said. He tossed the CD from the church service through the window onto the passenger seat.

Symone smacked her lips. "That's not the point, Antoine. Do you know league minimum is thirty-one grand?"

"Thirty-one grand?" Antoine said surprised. "You lying?"

"Nope. Dawg, state troopers make more than that coming out of training."

"It's only 2005. The WNBA's still new. You get in there and start dunking on fools, help increase those sales, the pay will go up soon enough."

"How 'bout I start by dunking on you and posting the video to Youtube. We'll probably sell out all the season tickets in Charlotte after people see that."

Antoine snatched the ball from Symone's hands and hustled to one of the vacant courts. Symone noticed his locs had grown since she last saw him a few years ago. Every time he turned his head, they swept across his broad shoulders like a broom cleaning dust off the front porch of a country style house on a dirt road. A slight pudge had also developed around his midsection, the result of not having to attend mandatory weight training sessions anymore.

Antoine looked Symone's way and gave a sly smile. "I'd like to see you try it."

"Don't tempt me." Symone returned the smile and ran up behind him.

Antoine used the friendly game of one on one basketball to have a serious talk with his younger sister.

"You know you leaving isn't going to fix anything," Antoine said as he shot a three point basket.

"Neither is me staying," Symone replied as she rebounded his miss shot. "She doesn't want me here, Ant. My presence may stress her out even more and stress me out, too. Besides, I can't be here and play ball too." Symone dribbled the ball to the far right corner and air-balled the fifteen-foot jumper.

"Ball comes second to family. You know that," Antoine said, chasing after the ball.

"We haven't talked in four years. She doesn't see me as family anymore."

Antoine bounced the ball hard into the ground with both hands and shouted, "Be better than her!"

"Honestly Ant," Symone sighed, "I'm tired of fighting. This is one I'm gladly giving to God."

"Yo Symone!"

Symone turned toward the voice and saw Janet 'Chief' Anderson making her way over to them. Symone smiled at her old friend and welcomed the break in her current conversation with Antoine.

"I was wondering if the number one draft pick was gonna stop by and check on us little people before she headed off to big time."

"Now you know you ain't nowhere near little, Chief."

Chief laughed at Symone's banter. "What's going on, Antoine."

"Not much," Antoine replied. He headed back to the court to shoot baskets and gave Symone and Chief the opportunity to speak privately.

Chief returned her attention back to Symone and patted her stomach. "Nothing wrong with staying healthy."

"Okay, healthy." Symone said sarcastically.

Symone swiveled her head from left to right nonchalantly. She realized the passing years increased

Chief's resemblance to *Winnie the Pooh* instead of decreasing it.

"Aye, I'm a big girl. Scraps for this two hundred pound body ain't gonna cut it."

"I hear that." Symone hugged Chief then continued, "Actually, I'm here 'cause my mom's in the hospital."

"What?"

"She had a stroke yesterday."

"Yo, I'm sorry to hear that."

"It's all good."

"So you sticking around for awhile?"

"Nah." Symone shrugged her shoulders. "My dad will probably move her back into the house until she gets to the point where she can take care of herself so she's in good hands."

"That's cool." Chief looked back toward the recreation center doors then returned her attention to Symone. "Well, I need to get practice started soon."

"Yeah, I heard you're coaching AAU summer league ball now."

"Sy," Chief smiled slightly, "some of these girls are the truth. They're just ten, eleven twelve years old but man, can they ball."

"Well, that's good. We gotta make sure the WNBA keeps growing, ya know."

"I feel you. I was hurt when the ABA folded but I think the world's finally ready to support a professional womens basketball team especially when we got ballers like you dunking and whatnot." Chief playfully nudged Symone. "Aye, why don't you stop in and say hi to the girls real quick?"

Symone looked down at her watch and replied, "I wish I could but I gotta get on the road. But wait," Symone walked over to her car and pulled a business card from her bag. She handed the card to Chief. "Stay in touch with me. Maybe we can set up a mini-camp or something for when the season's over."

Chief fiddled with the card between her fingers. "You got your own business card?"

"Whatever, dawg."

"Naw, I get it. You big time now." Symone blushed. "Aye," Chief began again, "I'm definitely gonna hold you to that mini-camp offer though."

"Do that."

"Good seeing you, Sy." Chief waved at Antoine, "See ya, Ant."

Antoine waved back and made his way over to Symone after Chief went inside the recreation center.

"What, I don't get a business card?" he joked.

Symone smacked her lips. "Shut up."

Antoine faked throwing the basketball at Symone's head before placing it in the backseat of the rental car. "So, you hitting the road now?"

"Yeah. I'm gonna call Aunt Betty and stop by and see her."

"All right, well, call me when you get there so I know you got there safe."

Symone gave her older brother a hug and replied, "I will."

"And think about what I said." Symone rolled her eyes as she got into the car. "I mean it," Antoine yelled.

Symone beeped the horn, pulled out the parking spot and threw up the peace sign as she drove off.

Chapter 6

"For the LORD your God is living among you.
He is a mighty savior....With his love, he will
calm all your fears." ~Zephaniah 3:17

THE GRAVEL CRUNCHED BENEATH the tires as
Symone pulled into the empty cemetery lot.

"Fifty minutes," she said glancing down at the
clock. "Fastest time to date."

Symone laid her head back on the headrest, closed
her eyes and let out a deep sigh.

"Okay," Symone said opening her eyes. "Okay."

She grabbed the folding chair and her Bible from
the passenger seat and exited the vehicle. Symone paused
in front of a huge oak tree that had the sign 'Freeman
Family Cemetery' tacked to it. She took off her sunglasses
and hung them on a rusty nail protruding from the sign.

Symone was careful to walk the worn path that
outlined each gravesite like a checkerboard pattern until
she reached her destination.

"Hey grandma." Symone walked up and knelt
before the headstone. She traced her finger over the
engraving, 'Audrey Freeman: Beloved Sister, Mother,
Grandmother: 1922-1996'. Symone smiled wearily at the
inscription underneath the dates; *'It takes a lifetime to learn
how to live. Share it in Bits 'N' Pieces'.*

"I know how much you like to see my eyes so I left my sunglasses at the sign." Symone placed her Bible on top of the headstone and set up the folding chair next to the grave. "You always said the eyes were the gateway to the soul," Symone sat down and finished, "I wanted you to see how much I still miss you. Even after all these years."

The mosquitoes began their attack before Symone could get comfortable in her chair but she came prepared. She reached into the cargo pocket on the right side of her patterned shorts and pulled out a miniature can of *OFF* bug spray. Symone sprayed a light mist over her arms and legs.

"Well, the devil's up to no good again," Symone began. "Ma's in the hospital. I went to go see her and—" Symone couldn't finish her statement. The emotional toil of the past few days events brought her to tears. "Sorry 'bout that," she said as she wiped her face with the back of her hands. "I've been an emotional wreck since coming to Virginia. It would make sense under the circumstances but I'm emotional for the wrong reasons." Symone removed the Bible from the headstone and placed it in her lap. Through more tears, she cried, "I'm focused more on what she thinks of me than her healing, Grandma. That's how bad the devil has my mind preoccupied with the past. But that's why I came to see you before heading back to Charlotte. Talking to you always helped me to get my mind back on track."

Symone opened the Bible and began to intercede to God on her mother's behalf by reading healing scriptures. She paused for a moment and smiled wearily as she thought back to the days when she and Antoine had bible study with their grandmother.

****

SYMONE TOOK TWO PILLOWS *from her grandmother's* *sofa and carried them into her grandmother's bedroom. Grandma* *Audrey was already kneeling at the bed and Antoine was to her* *right. Symone stacked the pillows on top of one another and pushed* *them up to the left side of the bed. Both Symone and Antoine* *crowded against Grandma Audrey like lineman huddled around a* *quarterback. They wanted to follow her every word as she read from* the *Illustrated Children's Bible Story book.*

"*Grandma,*" *Antoine's preteen voice cracked,* "*can you* *read us the story about Noah?*"

"*I wanna hear about Moses,*" *Symone said. Her sweet* *tone elevated in excitement,* "*and the parting of the Red Sea!*"

Grandma Audrey swiveled her head from left to right, *smiling at both of them.* "*I have a new story for you two tonight. It's* *about a man named Peter who walked on water.*"

"*A man can't walk on water, Grandma,*" *Antoine said* *doubtfully.*

"*Yeah huh,*" *Symone disagreed.* "*A man can do whatever* *he believes.*"

"*So if a man believes he can fly, he gon' fly?*"

"*Hush Antoine,*" *Grandma Audrey said.* "*It's not nice to* *mock your sister.*"

"*Sorry Grandma.*"

Symone stuck her tongue out at Antoine as Grandma *Audrey read the story. When she was finished, Antoine looked* *confused.*

"*I thought you said he walked on water?*" *Antoine asked.* "*He did.*"

"*But you just said he was sinking and Jesus had to save* *him.*"

"*That's right,*" *Grandma Audrey nodded her head in* *agreement.*

Antoine placed his hands on top his head. "*I'm confused.*"

"*Me too,*" *Symone said.*

Grandma Audrey knew they would miss the obvious. *Most adults never made the connection so she didn't expect Symone* *at eight and Antoine at twelve to make it either. She flipped to that particular part of the story and explained, "When Peter saw Jesus walking on the water, he asked Jesus if he could join him on the water, right?"*

"Yes," they both said in unison.

"And right here, it says that 'Peter went over the side of the boat and walked on the water to Jesus'. So he was walking on the water."

"So why did he start to sink?" Antoine asked.

Grandma Audrey slid the book closer to Antoine. Her frail, bony finger pointed to the passage. "Start reading right here."

Antoine scooted forward to the book and read, "But when he saw the strong wind and the waves, he became scared and began to sink'."

"When Peter first stepped out the boat," Grandma Audrey began, "he had his eyes on Jesus and as long as he kept his eyes on Jesus, he was walking on the water. Then he began looking at the wind and the waves and became scared. When he took his eyes off Jesus, he began to sink."

"Ohhh." The light bulb in Antoine's head turned on.

"So, what's the moral to the story?" Grandma Audrey asked.

Antoine shouted, "Always keep your eyes on Jesus!"

"Yes, but more importantly, don't let fear stop you from doing what you've already been blessed to do."

"Yeah, 'cause Peter was already walking on the water and then he got scared and stopped even though he was already doing it."

"That's right, Symone." Grandma Audrey nodded. "Many times, we're already doing great things in the world because we have our eyes on Jesus but then something happens and we get scared. We stop doing that great thing because we think we can't when really, we were already doing it before we got scared. So, what do we say about fear?"

Together, all three pointed to their hearts and shouted, "No fear lives here!"

****

SYMONE TURNED AND WATCHED as a silver Jaguar parked next to the Corolla. She smiled at her elegant eighty-eight year old great Aunt. Betty Nichols was the epitome of sophistication and grace. Her many years of working in the school district and service to the community highlighted her affluent status in the small town of Belvedere, North Carolina. She carried herself like royalty but she never boasted of her own merits. Like her older sister, Symone's late grandmother Audrey, Betty always kept God at the forefront of her life.

"Hello, Symone," Aunt Betty said in her distinct, high-pitched tone. She walked gingerly through the cemetery, holding up her green full-length sundress to avoid stepping on it with her yellow flats.

"Hey Aunt Betty." Symone stood up, hugged and kissed her on the cheek. "You didn't have to come out here. I told you I was gonna stop by."

"I know but you and your brother tend to make excuses when visiting. I wanted to make sure I saw you."

Symone smiled. With anyone else, she would have been offended but Aunt Betty knew her well.

"Here, have a seat." Symone offered her folding chair.

"No thank you. Those things can be difficult to get out of for an old lady like myself."

"You're not old, Aunt Betty. I bet if we walk down the street, people would mistake you for my sister."

Aunt Betty smiled and patted Symone on the arm. "How is your mother doing?"

"She all right. Dad said it happened because she stopped taking her blood pressure medicine."

"Oh Lord, when will we learn to take better care of ourselves?"

"I didn't even know she had high blood pressure. My dad, too."

"It's important to know your family history, Symone," Aunt Betty said. "Especially when it deals with health."

"Yeah, I know." Symone thought for a minute then asked a question she never imagined herself asking. "Aunt Betty, you know I'm gay, right?"

Aunt Betty was taken back by the question but didn't waver in her demeanor. "Yes, I know."

"And it doesn't bother you?"

"You are still a child of God regardless of who you love."

"You think Grandma would've felt that way?"

Aunt Betty moved beside Symone and placed her arm around her waist. "My sister, your grandmother, would've been proud of the woman you've become." She smiled as Symone blinked back tears.

"I was afraid to tell her," Symone confessed. "I didn't—I thought she might stop loving me like my mom did."

"Your mother didn't stop loving you."

"It feels like it. She wouldn't even let me kiss her—"

"She's still hurting, Symone. You both are. Running away is not going to make the pain go away."

"See, that's where everybody's wrong." Symone played with her long ponytail in frustration. "I didn't run away, Aunt Betty. I was forced out."

"I—"

Symone walked to her grandmother's headstone and knelt in front of it. "You know what I always wondered? If things would've turned out different if she was still around. I know ma would've talked to her about it and she would've listened to Grandma over my dad's family. I just wonder if—I don't know—if her presence, her words would've made a difference. Maybe even forced my mom to find acceptance, ya know. I just don't get why God allowed it to happen like this."

"God's plan is bigger than what we can see in the natural."

"Yeah," Symone sighed.

Aunt Betty twirled the loose fitting watch on her wrist and checked the time. "What time were you getting on the road?"

Symone looked at her watch. "I guess now. Charlotte's about a five and a half hour drive and it's going on four o'clock so—"

"Why don't you follow me back to the house and stay the night. Leave first thing in the morning after you're well rested."

"Aw, naw, I'm good, Aunt Betty."

"Thomas would love to see you," Aunt Betty mentioned. "He watched your basketball show the other night."

Symone looked at her confused then remembered, "Oh, the draft."

"Yes. He would be so pleased to have his great niece, the basketball star, eat dinner with him."

Symone laughed. Aunt Betty knew how to subtlety persuade her to stick around. "I haven't eaten since breakfast so dinner sounds good."

"Wonderful," Aunt Betty smiled in delight.

Symone gathered her things and guided Aunt Betty toward the cars. Once inside the vehicle, she texted Regina to let her know she was staying another night.

I've so missed this, Symone thought as she followed Aunt Betty down the road.

Part Two

Chapter 7

"The LORD is my shepherd; I have all that I need." ~ Psalms 23:1

SYMONE WALKED INSIDE THE lobby of Lez Bian Magazine. The logo on the wall behind the front desk was bold and written in Lucida calligraphy, **Lez Bian Magazine**. Through her former calligraphy business, Symone was familiar with this very elegant calligraphy style. She waved at the receptionist behind the desk who recognized her immediately. The receptionist smiled and motioned that she would make the call.

Symone sat down and studied the small company space. The walls were painted pure white and lightly decorated with seven black and white portraits of African American and Latina women. Shadowed behind each portrait was a brush stroke of bright color, representing the colors of the LGBT community.

Symone knew from her conversations with Regina that Lez Bian was a magazine geared toward the African American and Latina lesbian woman. Symone leafed through the copy on the table and saw that the company covered everything from news and entertainment to fashion, health and spiritual awareness. Lez Bian Magazine had a small subscriber list and only printed six editions a year but they hoped to expand as Charlotte's LGBT community continued to grow.

Symone glanced up and smiled as Regina swayed down the hall. Symone rarely saw Regina in her business attire and she had to admit, she loved the way the black and white plaid print quarter-length pencil skirt and pure black ruffle front blouse hugged Regina's petite frame. In college, Regina rarely wore high heels. Symone loved how the additional three inches elongated her muscular legs. Playing softball all four years of college kept Regina in great shape and Symone appreciated her athletically toned feminine figure in its purest form.

Regina began her internship at Lez Bian Magazine after she graduated college a year ago. Regina had not planned to remain in North Carolina, let alone Charlotte, especially since Symone had one more year of college before being eligible for the WNBA draft. They both believed it was the grace of God that the Charlotte Sting obtained the number one pick for the 2005 draft. It was then Regina felt her relationship with Symone was meant to be.

Symone's heart warmed when Regina held out her arms to hug her.

"Hey babe," Symone whispered into the nape of Regina's neck. Symone loved to nestle her head between Regina's jaw line and shoulder even though she knew it tickled Regina to do so.

Regina giggled when Symone's breath tickled her collarbone.

"Hey you," Regina said after a quick kiss.

"You look nice today," Symone said.

"Thank you." Regina stepped back and twirled like a runway model. "You know I can't work in the fashion department of a magazine without looking proper myself."

Symone smiled at Regina's comment then gave her another hug.

Symone's embrace expressed more than affection from absence. Regina felt Symone's need to talk or at the very least, the need of company, through the warmth of her grip. Symone would never say it but her eyes pleaded for Regina's company.

"I'm going to check and see if I can take lunch a little early, okay." After another quick kiss, Regina replied, "I'll be right back."

Regina was a very beautiful woman but her self-confidence was what Symone truly loved about her. Her sense of style evolved after her mother surprised her with a trip to Paris the summer after her sophomore year. After a month of exploring the beautiful city with her mother, Regina returned with a sense of purpose and more aware of what she wanted to do with her life moving forward. She changed her major to fashion design and her sense of style evolved along with it. Regina believed women felt better about themselves when they looked good and she wanted to help women gain that self-worth.

As Symone watched Regina walk back down the hallway, she noticed a light-skinned stud watching Regina too.

Symone was not naïve. She knew that new suitors approached Regina daily. Regina was upfront and honest, willingly divulging information about women and men who flirted with her. Symone was a little annoyed by all the attention Regina received especially since they lived almost five hours away from each other but Symone hoped it would die down after the first year. People always flocked to the new kid on the block but the hype wears down when there is no chance at getting play and no one else definitely had a chance. However, there were always a few who stuck around as 'friends' hoping they can slide in down the road. Symone knew she had to keep an eye on the light-skinned stud still checking Regina out from the corner of her eye. She definitely looked to be one of those types.

"Wow! If it isn't Symone Holmes in the flesh!" Symone looked up and found a beautiful milk chocolate woman standing before her. Regina stood a few feet behind her boss smiling.

The woman extended her hand. "I'm Rosalyn Parker, Editor and Chief and Regina's boss."

"Oh, nice to meet you," Symone said shaking her hand. "I hope I'm not getting her into any trouble for just popping up."

"Nonsense!" Rosalyn dismissed Symone's comment with the wave of her hand and added extra flare by snapping her head to toss her hair. "I'm a huge fan of women's basketball and when the Sting drafted you, I immediately became a season ticket holder."

Symone was caught off guard by Rosalyn's animated but warm personality. Rosalyn disregarded the unspoken rule of three feet of personal space but her outgoing yet calm approach dispelled the body's natural uneasiness response. The way Rosalyn accepted the slight gap between her two front teeth by welcoming Symone with a bright smile let Symone know she was very confident in presenting herself to others.

"That's awesome," Symone replied. "I'll do my best not to disappoint then."

"I'm not worried. We certainly can't do any worse than last year." Rosalyn turned to Regina and waved her over. "Go to lunch and take your time." She returned her attention back to Symone and said, "And if you feel the need to bring back some autographed—anything, feel free. We're all huge fans here."

Symone smiled, shook Rosalyn's hand again and followed Regina to the elevators.

"You boss is a trip," Symone said once they were out of earshot.

Regina smiled, "You have no idea. She has me cracking up all day long."

"Does she always where that much makeup though?"

"Unfortunately yes," Regina sighed. "Clinton, the guy who works in fashion with me, told her she was too beautiful and didn't need to wear all of that gunk but I think it's an insecurity issue with her."

"That woman insecure? I can't see it."

"You'd be surprise, Symone. Women use makeup to do more than just even out their skin tone. Dark spots, blemishes and acne aren't the only things we try and hide with foundation, tinted moisturizers or concealer cream."

EVEN THOUGH ROSALYN TOLD her to take her time, Regina did not want to take advantage of her kindness so she walked Symone to the sandwich shop across the street in the plaza.

After placing and receiving their orders, Symone and Regina found an empty table near the window facing the street.

"How's your mom?" Regina asked with no warning or warm up to the topic of conversation.

Symone shrugged and did not look up from her sandwich. "She's all right."

"Do they know how it happened?"

"She stopped taking her blood pressure medicine."

"Why?" Regina asked.

Symone shrugged again and took another bite of her sandwich.

"So she just stopped for no reason?"

"I guess."

Regina became annoyed Symone's short responses but she tried to overlook it due to the circumstances.

Regina reached over and gently squeezed Symone's hand. "You can talk to me baby. You need to let it out."

Symone leaned back in the chair and exhaled deeply. "I just don't want to talk about it right now. Let's talk about it when we get home."

Regina pulled her hand away and did not press the issue any further.

Symone felt Regina's frustration looming across the table so she changed the subject to try to lighten the mood.

"I ran into Chief while I was at the courts with Ant."

"How's she been?"

"She good. Coaching summer league AAU. She made me promise to do a mini camp for her team."

"Sam told me Kyra's coaching AAU, too."

Symone rolled her eyes at the mention of Kyra's name but Regina ignored the impolite gesture and continued, "Maybe you can do something with all the AAU teams."

"That'll take up too much time," Symone replied.

"Not if you do it as a separate camp instead of trying to do each team one on one."

"I'll get with Chief about it," Symone evasively agreed to the idea without really agreeing. "It might be better just to do a basketball camp for girls period, not just AAU players."

"That sounds like a great idea. You could get the AAU coaches to help and they could discover some new talent. I'll ask Sam to—"

"I said I'll get with Chief about it," Symone stated sternly, cutting Regina off abruptly.

Regina shot Symone a bone-chilling glare then decided to change the subject before she was tempted to hit Symone in her mouth.

"When are you heading back to Marian?"

Symone's left eyebrow perked up in suspicious wonder. "For what?"

"Final exams. Graduation."

Symone casually shrugged off the comment. "Being a future WNBA star from a small private school has afforded me some perks. My advisor spoke with my professors and two agreed to let me take my exam at a proctored testing site here in Charlotte. The other two, well, I have A's in those classes so they're not gonna make me waste my time with taking a final."

"And what about graduation?"

"I'm not going to graduation," Symone stated in a casual voice.

Her tone filled with growing agitation, Regina said, "Really Symone."

"Reggie, training camp starts next week and our first preseason game is in Connecticut on May 8th, the same weekend as graduation."

"And you're choosing basketball over walking across a stage to receive your diploma," Regina said with distain in her voice rather than a pressing question.

"Nobody who matters is coming anyway so why bother," Symone said sourly.

Regina subtly masked her hurt feelings behind a half-hearted smile as Symone returned to her sandwich, oblivious to the low blow she just delivered.

Chapter 8

"For I know the plans I have for you," says the
LORD. "They are plans for good and not for
disaster, to give you a future and a hope." ~
Jeremiah 29:11

IT WAS THE FIRST day of training camp and Symone
was surprised at how tired she was. The strength training
in the weight room was almost identical to the training
she did in college but with a few revisions. Mainly, the
insertion of weighted or medicine balls into most of the
drills. Symone felt her oblique, more commonly referred
to as 'love handles', tightening every time she threw the
medicine ball against the wall during the side lateral lung.

The endurance portion of the training shocked
Symone's system. The suicide drills were more extensive
than the normal suicides she ran in college. Symone
referred to suicide drills as 'down and backs'. You started
at one end of the court, the baseline. When the coach
blew their whistle, the team would run to the free throw
line then turn around and run back to the baseline. Then
they would turn back around and run to the half-court
line then back to the baseline. The next stop was the
opposite free throw line and back and finally you ran to
the opposite baseline and back. The new suicide drills the
pros introduced to Symone kept the same format in what

lines to stop at but instead of sprinting back to the baseline, the team had to back pedal back to the baseline. This was a difficult task once you reached and passed the half-court line. Symone felt the burn in her quadriceps and she was very happy that this exercise ended conditioning for the day.

Symone walked in the locker room with the rest of the players and gingerly sat down on the wooden bench. Her quads jumped in excitement.

"You doing okay, rook," Helen asked. Helen was a veteran power forward and according to her, the team's welcoming committee.

Symone wiped her face with a towel and answered winded, "Yeah, I'm good."

"Don't worry," Helen grinned, "the spasms usually stop after the third day."

"But you're definitely going to feel it when you wake up in the morning," Taneah added, "So be sure to ice up."

Taneah was also a veteran player but she was new to the Charlotte organization by way of the trade market. Symone was most excited about playing with her because Taneah's size reminded her of 'Chief' Anderson, her good friend from high school. Establishing a strong guard-center presence on the court would open up shots for other great shooters on the team.

Symone nodded and guzzled a twenty-ounce bottle of water in one sitting.

She took another bottle out of her bag when Helen cast a warning, "Slow down or you'll cramp up."

"Gotta—hydrate," Symone gasped in between breaths.

Helen pulled the bottle away from Symone's lips and replied, "Slow gulps."

Symone followed her instructions and felt her heart rate slowing down.

"How's your mom doing?" Gia asked unexpectedly.

"As good as someone who had a stroke can be, I guess," Symone answered.

Gia wrapped her arm around Symone's shoulder and said, "My dad had a heart attack last year so I know what you're going through." She motioned to the players in the locker room, "they were awesome in helping me through, especially since it was my first year in the league too."

"Yeah, we're like family here," Taneah said. "We look out for each other."

"Some of us are going out to shoot some pool later on," Helen chimed in. "Kinda like a team-bonding thing. You should come with us. Help get your mind off things."

"Thanks but—"

"Don't have us make it initiation for you new bread," Taneah cut Symone's decline of their invitation short.

Symone smiled and replied, "All right. Text me the address. I can't guarantee I'll play though." Symone flexed her right hand. "Depends on how good the trainer is in taking care of this thumb."

"She'll hook you up," Gia assured her.

"And don't think about backing out tonight either," Taneah said.

"Yeah, if you do, we'll have you make it up with running laps."

Symone laughed at Helen and replied, "Yeah right. I'll be lucky if I'm able to walk in here tomorrow."

Symone quickly changed clothes and left the locker room with her gym bag draped over her shoulder. She walked across the gym floor to the training room. She stood in the doorway while Candace, the team trainer prepared an ice bath for another player.

"I might need you to fix me one of those," Symone said jokingly.

Candace looked up, shook her head and smiled when Symone walked into the training room.

"What's so funny?" Symone asked as she hopped up on one of the padded tables.

"You just finished college season a month ago and you're in here needing treatment already?"

"Ha ha."

"I'm just saying—"

"Actually, if you think about it," Symone began her defense, "it makes sense that I'd have a few bumps and bruises *because* of the fact I've been playing longer."

"If you say so superstar."

"Superstar huh," Symone mumbled mockingly. "Okay. Really all I need is some ice for my thumb." Symone flexed her right hand repeatedly. "It's an old injury that never healed right so it swells up from time to time."

Candace walked over and gestured for Symone to show her the thumb. Symone reluctantly complied.

Candace ran her fingers along the sides of Symone's right thumb. She noticed a lump extended along the knuckle.

"This bone isn't aligned properly."

"Yeah, I know. I broke it my sophomore year of high school playing ball."

"The doctors didn't cast it right?" Candace asked as she headed to the cooler to fill a small plastic bag with ice.

"Uh, it's a little more complicated than that."

"What do you mean?"

"I never got a cast."

Candace paused from shoveling ice into the bag and glared at Symone suspiciously. Symone just laughed as she readjusted her position to get more comfortable before explaining her side of the story.

****

IT WAS THE DISTRICT finals and Symone thought it was fitting that they were playing against their district rivals, Mead High School.

"This is what championship ball is all about baby," Symone said to Chief as they walked onto the court for warm-ups. "The best against second best."

"They almost blew it losing to Connors though. They lucky Connors got blowed out by Hudson."

"That's why they're second best," Symone grinned.

Symone lined up on the right side of the court facing the home stands. Sitting three rows behind the team bench was Kidera with her best friend Trisha. Kidera felt someone looking at her and looked out onto the court. She locked eyes with Symone and Symone heart fluttered at Kidera's blushing smile.

"Symone! Ball!"

Symone turned in time to see the ball already in flight and headed in her direction. She put her hands up to protect her face and the ball bounced off the tip of her right thumb. Excruciating pain ran from Symone's thumb, up her arm all the way to her collarbone. The huge gasp by the spectators in the gym spoke volumes as Symone dropped to her knees clutching her arm.

"I heard that pop all the way across the floor," Sydney said as she knelt down next to Symone.

Coach Mason slammed his clipboard down on the bench and stormed out to the court with Brian, the athletic trainer, right on his heels.

Symone's breathing was labored as she stood to her feet and allowed Brian to check her injury.

"This doesn't look good, Coach," Brian said, shaking his head.

"Damn! Her thumb's fatter than a turkey sausage," Raquel, the backup point guard, squealed.

"I broke that shit, huh," Chief said in an easy tone.

"You think?" Sydney replied sarcastically.

The heat from his suppressed anger boiling turned Coach Mason's light-skinned face a flushed fuchsia color. "Why didn't you look before you threw the ball to her?" he yelled.

"Me? Man—"

"I can play," Symone finally spoke up. "Just give me some ice and splint it up."

"You're wincing every time I touch it," Brian pointed out.

"Stop touching it then." Brian glared at Symone who continued, "It's my RIGHT hand, Brian. I'm left-handed. I can play."

Brian looked around and saw a bucket of yellow softballs near the locker room entrance. He motioned for one of the players closest to the bucket to bring him a ball. He turned Symone's right hand right side up and placed the ball in her palm.

"Hold this." Symone gingerly wrapped her fingers around the ball. Brian shook his head no. He grabbed the ball and stated, "I meant grip it like this." Brian used just his fingers as he held the ball, palm down.

Symone gave him a condescending look but tried the task anyway. The ball fell and hit the court with a deafening thud. Brian nodded his head, happy to have made his point. "She can't even hold the ball, Coach."

"I can't palm a basketball either," Symone said smartly. "THAT didn't mean I couldn't play."

"Coach Mason—"

"I'm telling you I can play, Coach."

The horn sounded and the referees advised both coaches the game was about to begin.

Coach Mason rubbed his forehead with his forefinger and thumb. "Brian, get her some ice—"

"Coach—"

"Just do it!" Brian conceded and did as he was told. Coach Mason turned to Symone and said, "If I see this is not working, if you end up hurting us more than helping us do to this injury—"

"I got it but trust me, Coach. I'm good to go."

****

"SO YOU PLAYED WITH a broken thumb," Candace said when Symone finished her story.

"Yep and we won the game too." Symone smiled and carried on, "I even scored twelve points, broke thumb and all."

"You are a trainer's worse nightmare."

"Yes, I know but I'm sure pro teams wouldn't take the risk of me disfiguring myself for life."

"Probably, but I'm still lost. Did you ever go to a doctor to get it checked out?"

Symone nodded. "My mom took me to the emergency room after the game. They took X-rays and said my thumb had a break in two places but the joints were so badly swollen that they couldn't set the bones in the right place to cast it. They splinted it, told me to ice it three times a day, not to play ball and come back in a week."

"And I bet you didn't follow *any* of those rules did you?"

"We just won districts. There was no way I wasn't going to play ball but I iced it and my Coach had the trainer use an ace bandage to strap my arm to my chest during practices so I wouldn't risk doing more damage."

"So you didn't go back then?" Candace asked.

"I did go back." Candace stared at Symone suspiciously. "A month later," Symone finally admitted.

"A month?"

"We were in the middle of a championship run." Symone's voice elevated to a soprano's tone, indicating the importance of the delay. "If they would've put a cast on me I wouldn't've been able to play so I went back went we lost in the regional finals. But by that time, the breaks had started to heal incorrectly. The doctor said he would've had to break my thumb *again* to set the bones so they could heal properly."

Candace laughed. She knew before Symone finished that Symone did not let the doctors reset the breaks in her thumb.

"There was no way you were going to let them do it, were you?" Candace said.

"Why would I have them break my thumb again? It didn't hurt as much and I could still move it and hold things. And like I told Brian, I'm left-handed so I don't do much with my right hand to begin with."

"The stubbornness in some of you athletes is just amazing to me."

Symone said with a wide grin, "I thought you knew. We'd do anything for the game."

Chapter 9

"Trust in the LORD with all your heart; do not depend on your own understanding. Seek his will in all you do, and he will show you which path to take." ~ Proverbs 3:5-6

REGINA GLANCED OVER THE top of the sofa as she heard the front door open. She asked the person she was on the phone with to hold on as she greeted Symone.

"Hey baby," Regina said as Symone entered.

"Hey." Symone walked over to the sofa and kissed Regina softly on the lips. She licked the remnants of the strawberry lip gloss transferred to her through their kiss.

"I thought you were hanging with some of the players tonight?" Regina asked.

"I was but I changed my mind." Symone held up her right hand and showed Regina the ice pack strapped to her thumb with an ace bandage. "Besides, it's Wednesday and Bible study's tonight."

"It's online. You can watch it any time."

Symone sat quietly on the sofa with her eyes closed not responding. Regina shook her head and returned to her phone conversation.

"Hello?...Yeah, I'm back...No, she's not going anywhere...Making excuses but she's been staying pretty busy...we haven't found one yet."

Symone opened one eye and peeked in Regina's direction. "Who you talking to?"

"Sam."

Regina's best friend Samantha moved to Virginia to live with Kyra, her girlfriend, a year ago after Samantha graduated from college.

Symone grumbled under her breath but Regina could not make out what she said. Regina rolled her eyes and said to Sam, "Symone says hi."

The sofa was so comfortable, Symone was tempted to take a nap right there; however, Regina's phone conversation was not a soothing melody to fall asleep to.

Symone sat up and waved to get Regina's attention. She pointed toward the bedroom but Regina placed her hand on Symone's knee, pausing Symone's momentum.

"Here," Regina said handing the phone to Symone.

"I don't wanna talk to Sam."

"Just take the phone."

Symone let out a deep sigh and took the phone from Regina. "Yeah," she spoke with casual irritation.

"What–the–hell!" the voice on the other end shouted in short bursts. "You come to V-A and don't even call nobody?"

"It wasn't a pleasurable trip."

"I know it won't–Ooo, you lucky you in North Carolina right now." Symone slouched on the sofa as Kyra continued her rant. "I don't get you sometimes, Sy. I bet if you didn't run into Chief at Fairlawn, you wouldn't've told nobody nothing."

"Are you serious right now?" Symone asked as agitation grew within her. "We haven't talked in—"

"Fuck that!" Kyra exploded. "Your moms is laid up in the hospital. We go back too far for some beef to come in between serious shit like this. It's your moms, Sy."

Symone was speechless. She was surprised that Kyra felt that way and she was actually happy to know that her old friend still cared enough to be there when it mattered most.

"My bad, man," Symone replied in a calmer tone. "I didn't—I wasn't sure what to think. But you right, I should've called."

"Damn right." After a brief silence, Kyra asked sincerely, "So how she doing?"

With the tension subsided, Symone responded, "Okay I guess. I talked with my dad earlier today and he said she'll get to go home tomorrow."

"That's quick."

"Well, she's not at risk for getting worse. The big thing now will be the physical therapy to get her back where she can care for herself."

"Your pops gonna help her with that?"

"Oh yeah," Symone said assuredly. "He's gonna check to see if his insurance will cover it. My mom was only working part-time so she didn't have medical coverage."

"I thought they were divorced," Kyra said perplexed.

"They are but he pays some of the bills at her apartment so he's trying to see if that'll qualify him as her caregiver. Some loophole one of his co-workers told him about."

"For real?"

Symone nodded as if Kyra could see her. "Yeah. I think he has to show that he covers more than half of her living expenses or something like that. I don't know all the details but if he qualifies, my mom's medical can be covered by his insurance even though they're not legally married anymore."

"That's what's up. Hopefully, that'll work out for him."

"Yeah, me too."

The awkward silence finally seeped into their conversation and Symone was not sure what topic to bring up to rid of it.

"Well, look um, I'm just getting in from basketball practice—"

"The first time we talk in almost two years and you really gonna cut this convo short." Symone sighed aloud. "Nah, it's cool," Kyra replied. "Baby steps, right?"

"Yeah."

"All right but you better call me if anything changes with your moms."

"I will—and thanks." Symone handed the phone back to Regina and resumed her previous venture in escaping to the bedroom.

Symone paused in the doorway of the master bedroom. Even though she and Regina bought the house together, Symone still felt like she was a guest in the home. Regina's sense of style was contemporary and clean, which always made Symone feel she was leaving something out of place any time she moved it. Symone was not opposed to Regina's style especially when it dealt with clothes. During Symone's junior year of college, there was an increase in interviews about her impending professional career with the WNBA. Regina spent her whole paycheck at *Express Men*, purchasing Symone a new wardrobe consisting of dress shirts, dress pants, ties, sweaters and dress shoes to give Symone a more professional look. "The WNBA may be just basketball to you," Regina told her, "but the WNBA is a business and you are the product, the brand. You have to present yourself in a way that is marketable to the consumers and other business organizations. That's the importance of brand imaging."

Symone understood completely from a business aspect but she did not expect to have to keep up that same image in her own home. Every bit of their bedroom said modernistic except the small corner near the window. Contrasting heavily with the elegant bedroom set was a metal framed school desk Symone bought at a yard sale for five dollars. The desk had a manila hardwood top that had hearts, shooting stars and 'Kasey loves Jamie' etched in it. The metal base and legs were tarnished from excessive weather exposure. Symone used the desk to house her laptop, the hardwood top concealed the portable computer inside when not in use. It was her own private sanctuary in a sea of futuristic ambience.

It was nearly 7pm so Symone skipped the shower and sat down at the desk. She wanted to lie down but Regina always nagged her about her lack of consideration. She didn't like it when Symone threw the ice bags in the trashcan. Sometimes the water seeped through the bags and stained the carpet in the bedroom. Then there was the issue of Symone resting in bed before taking a shower. According to Regina, the stench of basketball sweat settles into the comforter, causing her migraines in the middle of the night. Symone shoulders slumped as she exhaled loudly. Peace was what she was searching for but she could not seem to find it even in the most obvious place.

Symone removed her laptop from its hidden compartment and turned it on. She tapped her fingers on the top of the desk as she waited for the laptop to load. She typed the church's website into the URL field and clicked on the Wednesday night online bible study tab.

"Five and a half minutes," Symone read aloud from the computer screen. "Hmm."

She used the free time to open a new tab and searched for 'serene locations in Charlotte, NC'. Symone was coming up empty in her search so she continued to rummage through the internet sites even after bible study began.

Regina strolled into the room, pausing at the foot of the bed to listen to the bible study sermon emitting from the speakers. Regina moved to gather her bible but noticed that Symone's bible was still resting on the nightstand.

"What are you doing?" Regina asked with tensed wonder.

"Oh, um, I got caught up in searching for some places here in Charlotte where I can go clear my head."

"You're kidding, right?"

Symone looked at her confused. "Why would I be kidding? In V-A, I had Waterside and at Marian I had Cooper's Lake. Now I need to find a solace place here."

"I should be your solace place!" Regina shouted.

"My solace place can't be a person," Symone said mockingly. "That's why they call it solace *place*."

"Don't get smart with me."

"Why do you always do this, Reggie?"

"Me? You're the one who refuses to talk to me!"

"I'm not *refusing* to talk to you. I don't know how. You know this already. It's been four years. Why you pushing me on this now?"

"Because I've never seen you this disturbed before. Maybe I should've forced the issue sooner but you've always bounced back in a day or less." Regina walked over and sat on the side of the bed that faced Symone. "I know how important rectifying your relationship with your family means to you and I wish you'd let me help you through this."

"I just don't want you caught up in my family drama."

"You say you want to marry me one day, right?"

"Of course."

"Then that means this becomes my family drama, too."

"Yeah but—"

"No battle is won with just one soldier," Regina stated plainly. "You need an army to fight the good fight with you."

"You're right but strong soldiers—"

"Wait, you don't think I'm strong enough?" Regina asked offended.

"You didn't even let me finish."

With challenge in her voice, Regina replied, "Fine. Finish."

Symone knew she should have quit while she was ahead but unfortunately, she never learned to listen to her inner voice.

"Honestly, I *don't* think you're strong enough to handle this. That's why I'm carrying the burden all on my shoulders. To protect you from getting hurt."

Regina was taken back. "Wow."

"See, I knew—"

"Don't say you knew I was going to take that the wrong way because there's no other way to take that except the way you put it."

Symone tried to think of a good rebuttal but she knew Regina was right. There was no way to fix calling someone a weak person.

"Well," Regina exhaled loudly, "now that I know what you think of me, I'll leave you to getting your strength from staring at a body of water."

"Reggie—"

Regina snatched away from Symone's grasp and hurried out the room. Symone knew she hurt Regina's feelings but she felt she had to be honest in why she would not accept her help. To have a weak solider fight for you is worse than fighting alone because once that weak person breaks down, you have to carry them through the battle. Symone did not believe she had enough strength to fight her family and carry Regina as well. It would just be too much to bear.

Chapter 10

"But blessed are those who trust in the LORD and have made the LORD their hope and confidence."
~ Jeremiah 17:7

THE DIFFERENCE BETWEEN BEING conceited and being confident is that a conceited person trusts in their own abilities, believing that it's by their own hands that they are successful. A confident person knows that they're successful because of God's grace coupled with their faith in His word.

The bible study message still resonated in Symone's mind as training camp ended for the day. The soreness in her body started to subside but her mind was still plagued with emotional scars and mental inflammation. Symone stared into the half midst mirror above the sink in the locker room. The distorted image looking back at her almost made her heart stop. For the first time, Symone saw her mother in her. The round eyes, the wide nose, the baby moles peppered on her cheeks. All her life she had been told she resembled her father and grandmother, not her mother. Now that she was growing into a woman, she started to realize that there was more of her mother in her than she thought.

"We missed you the other night," Helen said. Her dirty blonde hair carried a lavender scent from her shampoo.

"Yeah, I got home and crashed," Symone replied. "Next time though."

"I'm gonna hold you to that."

Symone thought about getting dressed but decided against it. She needed to clear her head and nothing worked better than a few rounds of shooting baskets.

"I've always heard of players that stayed in the gym after practice for hours on end but I never actually seen one do it until now."

Symone smiled at Candace as she approached. Symone continued shooting from the free throw line, making five in a row.

"Now I see how you stay perfect from the line."

"I actually don't practice to shoot better." Candace looked confused so Symone corrected, "I mean, I do but shooting helps me keep my mind clear from outside issues."

"Still thinking about your mom?" Candace asked as she rebounded the ball.

Symone ignored the question and responded, "Shooting is my therapy. The free throw line is the only time on the court that play is slow enough for a player to concentrate on mechanics and technique." Symone made another basket and continued, "I close my eyes and take a deep breath. Then I just stand here holding the ball with my eyes closed." Symone demonstrated as she carried on, "Some have the ritual of twirling the ball or dribbling it. Me, I just stand here holding it. I allow my mind to go blank and then I picture myself making the shot. I actually envision the ball going through the hoop. Once I get that image in my head, I open my eyes and shoot." Symone made another basket.

"And you can do all that in under ten seconds?"

"I've been doing this since—I can't even remember when so it doesn't take long for me to get that vision in my head. I can actually do it in a matter of seconds."

Candace was impressed with Symone's work ethic and her ability to use basketball as a form of therapy to overcome whatever hardships she faced. In being a physical therapist, Candace always found herself lending an ear to players who could not help but vent about everything from the league, coaches, other players and family life. She knew holding in emotional pain was not healthy so the fact that Symone found a way to cope with hers was enlightening to Candace.

"The first preseason game is inching closer," Candace said. "Feeling nervous yet?"

"Honestly no," Symone said, finally missing a shot. "It's still over a week away, though. I don't think I'll feel the nerves 'til we either board the plane or when I walk into the gym."

"The first game's at Connecticut?"

"Yep. I'm still getting used to the thought of all the travel we'll be doing. Even being here in Charlotte is an adjustment."

"How are you and your partner liking it here?" Candace asked.

Symone paused before beginning her ritual at the free throw line again. With a slight raise of her left eyebrow, she said with a sarcastic undertone, "My partner?"

"You *do* have a girlfriend, right?" Candace asked unsure.

"Yeah but why didn't you just say girlfriend?"

"Oh," with a bashful laugh, Candace replied, "I don't know."

Symone shrugged off Candace's inability to defend her choice of words and responded to the original question. "She's been here for almost a year so she's already comfortable."

"Oh."

Symone could hear the confusion in Candace's tone so she explained, "Regina was a year ahead of me in college so she graduated last year. She took an internship with a magazine company here in Charlotte. We just lucked out that the Sting drew first pick this year and I was chosen."

"She must be something else."

"Who?"

"Your girlfriend."

"Why you say that?"

"You've been here two weeks and the first time I've seen you smile was just now. You *literally* lit up talking about her."

Symone blushed. "Yeah, she um—she affects me like that."

"That's good. We should all know love like that." Candace paused before reluctantly stating, "I always seem to fall for the girls—and I do mean girls—who want to see how many women they can sleep with."

Symone suspended her shooting and looked at Candace inquisitively. Candace's kinky twists elevated her personality with their spikiness and bounce. Symone saw that her body was well toned but more like a personal trainer, not an athlete. The light brown streaks in Candace's twists added a nice contrast to her toasted almond skin tone. If Symone was not in love with Regina, Candace was a woman she would definitely pursue.

"Yeah, unfortunately there are some studs out there that have the mannish 'bag 'em and tag 'em' mentality but not all. You'll find someone who'll appreciate you. It's that whole 'sifting through the weeds to find that one flower thing'."

"You're right. I just wish someone plowed my lawn so I didn't have to go through so many weeds."

They both laughed and Symone found herself relaxing in Candace's presence.

"I really admire you Symone."

"Really? Why?"

"Do you know how hard it is to be an out lesbian as a professional athlete?"

"I never really thought about it. I've been out since high school, ya know." Symone placed the ball back on the ball rack and walked over to the bleachers. Candace followed and sat down beside her. "I don't know any other way to be."

I know but that's huge, especially for a stud."

"Why you say that?"

"Because the way you carry yourself says lesbian."

"Wow, thanks," Symone said with playful banter.

Candace laughed. "No, I meant that it's not hard for people to guess that you're a lesbian as opposed to me or your girlfriend who dresses more feminine."

"Oh ok. Yeah, you're right about that. But you know what really gets me?"

"What?"

"People who think I wanna be a man because I dress in mens clothes." Candace could not hide the guilty look on her face that disclosed she thought the same thing. "Not you too!" Symone teased.

"Why else would you wear mens clothes?"

"'Cause they're comfortable. Who wants to walk around in heels all day? Got corns the size of gumballs growing on your pinky toe."

"Eww!"

"But for real, I love being a woman. We are the most beautiful creatures God ever created. We are strong enough to endure the pain of childbirth, more than once but sensitive and loving enough to soothe a crying baby. We can bum it out in jogging pants, a tank top and a do-rag on our heads then *turn* heads when wearing a strapless form fitting dress."

"We are bad," Candace said with gleaming confidence.

"Yes we are. Now why would I want to relinquish this power? I love everything about being a woman. And being a woman that loves women—" Symone whistled in delight.

"Oh, trust me," Candace smiled, "I get it. Wow."

"What?"

"I just—never would've thought."

"You thought I'd be some manly man stud, didn't you?"

"No—well…"

"I'd have you to know I'm actually the one who does most of the" Symone used air quotes, "'womanly things' around the house."

"Like what?"

"I do most of the cooking and since my wardrobe has become more exquisite, I do my own laundry."

"And your girlfriend?"

Symone thought for a moment. "She's big on cleanliness, I mean huge. Even with the cars."

"So she cleans the cars?"

Symone nodded. "And I happily toss her my keys, too."

Candace laughed. "Sounds like you two have a fifty-fifty relationship."

"Oh yeah, I mean, I think relationships have to be that way to be successful."

"Look at you. Keep talking like that and you can't categorize yourself as a stud anymore."

Symone rolled her eyes. "I so hate labels because of that. And that's why I don't hang with a lot of studs. Don't call me 'homeboy', 'man', 'bruh' or anything close to that."

Candace laughed aloud to Symone's comment. "I know a number of studs who refer to themselves as such."

"If that's how they get down then cool but I'm not a dude and I'm not trying to be one, period."

Chapter 11

"Faith is the confidence that what we hope for will actually happen; it gives us assurance about things we cannot see." ~ Hebrews 11:1

SYMONE CHEWED ON HER pinky nail as she paced the living room floor. She received a call from her Uncle Ward earlier in the day. He was in Charlotte and wanted to stop by and visit. Uncle Ward was one of Symone's fathers' older brothers and even though Symone was not close to that side of her family, Uncle Ward stayed in touch over the years. He was an independent trucker, delivering cargo all across the country. Symone found the timing of his visit to Charlotte more than a coincidence but she was excited to sit down and catch up with him.

Symone heard the rustling from the truck cab as it screeched to a halt in front of the house. Symone looked out the living room window and laughed wearily under her breath. Uncle Ward was already out of his cabin and flirting with the neighbor across the street.

"This guy." Symone stepped outside her front door and yelled. "Uncle Ward! I'm over here!"

Uncle Ward waved Symone off without even turning around.

"Really?" Symone thought for a minute then smiled. "How's Aunt Maddy doing?" Symone shouted with the smile in her voice. "And the kids, they good?"

It didn't take long for Symone's neighbor to get the hint and excuse herself from Uncle Ward's presence. Symone flashed a huge grin to try to compress the bitter glare Uncle Ward shot her before crossing to her side of the street.

"Why you blocking?" Uncle Ward said with a hint of hip-hop swag.

"Please don't try and sound like today's youth," Symone smirked. "It's not a good look on you."

Uncle Ward playfully rolled his eyes and wrapped his arm around Symone's shoulders. "Show me your castle, niece."

Uncle Ward whistled, impressed with the tan, powdered blue and light green modern-style living room set. "Swan-ky." His deep southern draw delivered more volume to his baritone voice.

"Yeah, it's a little too upscale for my taste but Regina likes it so—"

"This couch is hard as bricks," Uncle Ward said as he took a seat on the light green leather sectional sofa. "Cots in the army were more comfortable than this."

"They have high density foam in them for added support," Symone explained. "You know I need something firm to help my back."

"And what's this?" Uncle Ward tapped the table attached to the side of the sofa.

Symone smiled, "It's called a veneer tray. She uses it as a food tray when guests come over."

"So it's what you use to serve the food?"

"Yeah."

"Well hell, why didn't you just say so?"

Symone laughed aloud. She walked toward the kitchen and asked, "You want something to drink?"

"A beer would be fine."

"I don't have beer."

"How 'bout a soda pop?"

"Don't have that either."

Uncle Ward turned around and stared at Symone. "What kind of people don't carry beer or soda pop?"

"You know I don't drink nann one of those, Uncle Ward." Symone replayed her last statement in her head and laughed to herself. It was only when she was around her North Carolina family that she uttered her own southern idioms.

Symone poured her uncle a glass of pomegranate lemonade and grabbed a bottle of water for herself.

"You have any friends who looking for a sugar daddy?" Uncle Ward asked after taking a long swig of the lemonade.

"You kidding me, right?"

"I know you into women and all but I know you gotta friend or two who likes men or both. It don't matter. I'm just looking to have a little fun while I'm in town."

Symone stared at her uncle in disbelief. She could not believe he was asking her to facilitate his adulterous acts.

"You do realize that Aunt Maddy is—*my Aunt*. I know I don't participate in family functions and most of the family may not even acknowledge me as family but she's still—family."

"By marriage," Uncle Ward said.

"So?"

"I'm your family by blood."

"Again, I say so?"

"So your alliance lies with me, not her."

Symone thought for a minute then replied, "I can honestly say that's the most ignorant statement I've ever heard you say and I've heard you say a lot of ignorant stuff."

Uncle Ward smacked his lips and adjusted his groin area as he shifted positions on the sofa. Symone made a mental note to have him wash his hands before touching anything else.

"Don't get me wrong. I love Maddy with all my heart but things have been rough for a few years."

Symone noticed the change in Uncle Ward's tone. He was distressed about something so she asked, "What's going on?"

"Cassie told us she liked girls two years ago."

"Lil Cas?" Symone said in awe. Cassandra was Uncle Ward's oldest daughter but she was three years younger than Symone. They lived in Hampton, which was twenty minutes across the bridge from where Symone grew up in Norfolk so the two did not hang out much when they were growing up.

Uncle Ward nodded. "Supposedly, she fell in love with a senior in high school." Symone did not like the insinuation behind 'supposedly' but she let him continue without interruption. "Cassie was only a sophomore back then. Maddy was livid and never let up on Cassie so when she finally graduated, Cassie followed the girl to Alexandria."

"Whoa, wait. Cas moved with the girl?"

Uncle Ward nodded through another gulp of lemonade. "Packed her stuff and was gone as soon as she received her diploma."

"Wow. And Aunt Maddy won't give you any play 'cause Cas moved to Alexandria to live with her girlfriend?"

"Your Aunt isn't doing her wifely duties because like your father, I refused to listen to our family when they wanted us to cut Cassie off. She's still mad at me after all this time."

Symone stared at her Uncle stumped by his last statement. "What do you mean, like my dad?"

"Just what I said." Uncle Ward noticed the bewildered look on Symone's face and uttered with a surprised scoff. "Huh, you don't know."

"I am completely lost," Symone admitted.

Uncle Ward settled into the stiff sofa as much as he could. He draped his arms across the headrests and said, "After I tell you this story, you'll be buying me that beer and maybe even sharing one with me."

Symone listened intently as Uncle Ward told her that her mother sought advice from her father's family about her homosexuality. The family's advice was for Paula to put Symone out and disown her. Paula told Frederick she wanted to go along with the family's decision but he was against it and refused to let her do it.

"Wow," Symone said shocked. "I—I didn't even know he knew."

"Oh yeah, he knew."

"No, I mean, every time he was around, my mom shut down—like she was hiding it from him."

"That's because he put his foot down about you. He told her he didn't care what the family said. They weren't putting you out and he didn't want to hear anymore about it."

"Are you serious?" Symone was dumbfounded. She knew her father to be a quiet, passive man. Nothing Uncle Ward said matched her father's personality.

"You know I am." Uncle Ward rubbed his stubble beard in satisfaction. "That was the first time in a long time I saw my baby brother stand up for something and it made me proud." He leaned forward and said in a comforting tone, "He said to your mom, 'she's our daughter. What are we going to do, stop loving her?' Now that's a man I wanted to be like."

Symone was in awe. She never knew her father fought for her. She didn't think anyone did.

"Why didn't he say something to me?"

"You know Fred. Reserved, always keeping to himself. Hell, you got that same trait and I know for damn sure he didn't know how to come to you and start the conversation. Next thing he knew you were moving out and—"

"I moved out 'cause ma was making it too hard for me to live there. Between the cold stares and the snide comments, I just couldn't take it no more."

"Hmm," Uncle Ward grunted through a sip of his lemonade. "I don't think he knew about that. He told me he thought you moved out to be with your girlfriend."

Symone was still trying to process the information. "I just—I wish he would've—maybe I should've said something."

"That's water under the bridge now."

"It's not. They gotta divorce because of me—"

"No they didn't." Uncle Ward dismissed the statement with the wave of his hand. "Your parents had problems bigger than you liking girls, Sy. Don't put their marriage on you."

"Yeah but—"

"No buts. What happened between them was because of them and it ain't nobody fault but theirs."

Symone sat back and exhaled loudly. She massaged her forehead just above her eyebrows to stop the onset of a headache.

With a humorless half grin, Uncle Ward stated confidently, "You look like you ready for that beer now."

"This is the *very* reason why I don't drink, family."

Chapter 12

"I am leaving you with a gift—peace of mind and heart. And the peace I give is a gift the world cannot give." ~ John 14:27

SYMONE BOUNCED HER LEG nervously as she and Regina waited outside for their name to be called.

"Relax honey," Regina whispered.

"I'm good," Symone uttered softly.

Regina leaned in and kissed Symone on the cheek. Symone looked around nervously.

"It's fine, Symone. This is a gay friendly restaurant."

Regina saw the tension escape through Symone's shoulders like steam rising from a hot frying pan placed in cold water.

"I should've known you'd be the first to arrive."

Symone and Regina both turned to the voice that came from behind them.

"Hey Zen," Regina said. She stood and embraced her before introducing them. "Symone, this is Zen. She's one of the writers at the magazine."

Symone took Zen's hand and shook it aggressively. She immediately recognized her as the light-skinned stud that was checking Regina out the time Symone stopped by the office.

"Zen?" Symone repeated with skepticism.

"It's short for Zenadia. I'm Dominican," Zen shared, rubbing her hands together nervously. She turned to Regina and said, "Wow, you look gorgeous. I don't think I've ever seen you with your hair up."

Regina averted eye contact with Symone, gently patted her updo and replied, "Thank you. You're not looking too bad yourself. I don't think I've seen you in all white before and linen, too."

"With the class of women I'm hanging with tonight, I figured I'd better step it up a bit."

"You know Anita's still going to clown you about that green shirt though."

Zenadia tugged at the white linen button down shirt she wore over top the green T-shirt. "Maybe if I button it up, she's not going to notice it."

Symone coughed to break the dialogue. Regina smelled the bravado secreting through Symone's pores. She displayed the same macho demeanor when Regina used to date Melissa back in college. The territorial gesture was overkill but Regina took pleasure in seeing that Symone still felt the need to make it known that she was her girl.

"How long have you two been waiting?" Zen asked.

"Maybe ten minutes," Regina replied, "but I knew it might be a bit of a wait for a party of eight."

"Eight?" Zen repeated surprised.

"I wasn't sure who all was coming so I rounded up." Regina smirked under her breath and continued, "You know Anita and Devon never RSVP for anything but pop up like they're the ones hosting the party."

"Or like the party was thrown in their honor."

"True!" Regina laughed with Zen.

Symone grew agitated with their one on one exchange so she interjected and asked Zen, "So where's your date?"

"I'm stag tonight."

"Zen has this rule," Regina began with a hint of humor, "She never brings a woman on a group date unless their exclusive."

Zen shot a playful glare at Regina and explained, "For some reason, certain women—"

"Only the ones you date," Regina blurted out.

"Obviously. It's like I'm a magnet for crazy, over-committed, suffocating women." Symone rolled her eyes as Regina and Zen shared another laugh.

"I wanna laugh too." Symone's statement dripped with sarcasm.

"Oh right. It's like these women take meeting my friends as a sign that the relationship is moving toward moving in together or marriage or something when really all I want to do is hang out and chill."

"One girl actually cried when Zen introduced her to me." Regina laughed and carried on, "She was hugging Zen shouting, 'YES, YES!' like Zen had just proposed."

"I'll never make that mistake again."

"A magnet for sure," Symone replied with as much sarcasm as her last statement. "Where do you find them?"

"Stewart, part of eight," echoed from the intercom.

"That's us," Regina said and motioned them to the door.

Symone was happy to hear that their table was ready. Zen's subtle flirting with Regina boiled under Symone's skin at a rapid pace.

There were two tables pushed together to meet the group's attendance of eight. No chairs were placed at the ends so if everyone showed up, each person would end up sitting across from another. Regina sat one seat in from the end while Symone occupied the end seat. Zen took the liberty of sitting directly across from Regina.

Anita and another woman joined the three just as the waiter appeared to take their orders for drinks and appetizers.

"Symone, this is my good friend Anita," Regina introduced.

"And this is Cato everyone," Anita announced to the table. "A *friend*," she stated directly at Regina. Regina just smiled.

Symone stood to her feet and shook hands with both Anita and Cato.

Anita reminded Symone of Regina's boss, Rosalyn. She was very assertive and animated in approaching new people. Her confidence beamed through the form fitting black dress that also complimented her tall frame and voluptuous curves. Symone purposely looked Anita in the eyes to avoid staring at the deep V-neckline that accentuated her cleavage. Even the mesh fabric covering the exposed area did little to hide breasts that could give Pamela Anderson a run for her money.

"Ooo, I love the chivalry," Anita squealed when Symone stood up. "I bet you open car doors and walk closest to the street down the sidewalk, don't you?"

"She does," Regina answered proudly.

Anita shifted her eyes to Cato and replied, "This one's still learning."

Cato grunted under her breath and sat down in the nearest chair, the end seat across from Symone. Anita remained standing in front of her chair that was on the other side of Zen.

"Um—" Anita sung aloud.

Cato looked over Zen's head and saw Anita still standing. She grinded her teeth, stood to her feet and pulled out Anita's chair. Cato then took a seat next to Anita at the other end.

"Like I said, still learning," Anita sighed.

Symone could tell by the way Anita carried herself that she was in her late twenties, early thirties; however, Cato was around her age. Symone didn't have many masculine female friends and Cato's black leather vest and motorcycle helmet caught Symone's attention.

"You ride?" Symone asked the obvious question.

Cato nodded. "Ninja Kawasaki 650r," she tapped the top of her helmet and unleashed a gold-capped tooth grin, "It's my baby."

The waiter returned with their drinks and assured that their appetizers were on the way. As he walked away, two other women approached the table.

"'Bout time you showed up," Anita said to the dark-skinned femme. "I thought I was going to have to do this interrogation on my own."

The older stud dressed in all black escaped for a brief moment to hunt down the waiter and place their drink orders. Devon, shining in a bright red blazer, stayed behind with the group. "Blame Tanesha," she said. She walked around the table clockwise, starting with Zen, supplying everyone with hugs. "She takes longer than me getting ready to go somewhere."

"I LOVE the hair," Regina exclaimed as they exchanged hugs. "And those rainbow rimmed frames are too cute!"

"Thank you, thank you," Devon blushed. "But these twist outs were giving me hell, girl."

"You rocking it though."

Devon put her fist in the air and said, "Yes, I'm still holding strong to the natural hair movement. And this must be Symone," Devon said once she reached the end of the table. "I'm Devon."

"Nice to meet you."

Devon studied the seating arrangements and shook her head in displeasure.

"Zen, you need to come to this side of the table so Tanesha and I can sit across from Symone."

"Why can't the two of you sit right there?" Zen pointed at the two vacant seats next to Regina.

"Because I can't talk to Symone if I can't see her."

"That's a lie."

"Get up," Devon ordered.

Zen exhaled loudly but moved her glass across the table. Symone wanted to object to Zen sitting next to Regina. She wanted to keep her eye on the woman who was flirting with her girlfriend but did not want to cause a scene.

"Now isn't this better?"

"Baby, you playing musical chairs again?" Tanesha asked. She kissed Devon on the cheek and pulled out her chair for her to sit down.

"See," Anita said to Cato. "Learn from these mature studs on how to treat a woman instead of seeking advice from your wannabe thug nation friends please."

Cato smacked her lips and pretended to read the menu.

Tanesha introduced herself as she took her seat across from Symone. "I'm Tanesha everybody."

"And I'm Clinton."

Everyone turned to the brown haired, blue-eyed male standing at the head of the table.

"You made it!" Regina gasped in delight. She slid back her chair and gave Clinton a warm hug.

"Of course!" Clinton exclaimed. "I wouldn't miss hanging with you bits for the world!" He stepped back and admired Regina's outfit. "Ooo! I see you took my advice and went with the ruffles."

Regina smoothed her hands down the heather gray pencil skirt and flirtatiously played with the flat folded ruffles that ran down the left seam. "Yes, darling. This skirt jazzes up this top to a T."

"Just a touch of sexy flare." Regina and Clinton shared in a brief laugh then Clinton turned his attention to the table. "Now where am I sitting?"

Regina eyes landed at the last vacant seat next to Zen at the far end of the table. Clinton gave Regina a sour look then summoned the nearest wait staff to the table.

"Yes, I need those items down there moved here," Clinton told the waiter.

Everyone watched as Clinton positioned himself at the head of the table near Symone. He tipped the waiter five dollars for accomplishing the move without a challenge.

"Symone," Clinton began softly, "do you mind switching seats with my Regina bear?"

Before Symone could respond, Regina answered, "She's left-handed Clinton so I always let her have the end." Symone caught herself from responding negatively to Regina's choice of words as she carried on, "It keeps her elbow from jabbing me while we're eating."

"Ooo, stay where you are then, honey."

Symone pretended to wipe her mouth, using the napkin to cover the discontent on her face of the people Regina had surrounded herself with while living in Charlotte.

The appetizers finally made it to the table and Symone was ecstatic. She planned to keep her mouth stuffed with food as a deterrent from saying something out of line to Regina's eccentric group of friends.

Symone bowed her head and said grace over her chicken quesadillas. When she opened her eyes, she noticed everyone at the table staring at her. "What?" she said with a bit more attitude than she expected.

"The waiter wants to go ahead and take our order for the entrée," Regina said quickly.

Symone glanced up at the waiter who did not seem to mind whether she placed her order now or later.

Once the orders were placed for the main course, the discussions began. After listening to Anita, Devon,

Clinton and Regina converse for ten minutes, Symone decided to break the monotony of their catty chatter.

"So how did ya'll meet?" Symone asked no one in particular. "I know Zen and Clinton work with Reggie but—"

"Reggie?" Devon repeated with glee. "That is so cute!"

"Isn't it?" Anita agreed.

"She's been calling me that since the day we met."

"Aww!" Clinton, Anita and Devon cooed in unison.

Symone closed her eyes and prayed for instant relief. "Yeah, so how did ya'll become friends again?"

"Well," Anita began, sounding like a high school valley girl, "Devon and I have been friends since middle school. We were both cheerleaders on the junior varsity cheerleading squad."

"Yay!" Devon shouted with a fist pump.

"Cheerleaders, of course."

Regina heard the hint of sarcasm in Symone's voice but Anita and Devon didn't seem to notice it.

"Anyway," Devon picked up where Anita left off, "We may not be cheering anymore but we'd die before letting our bodies look like we belong on the *Biggest Loser* so we go to the gym five times a week."

Anita sipped her lemon-flavored water and added, "Regina was at the gym the same time we were. We saw how well she maintained that sexy physique and knew she would be the perfect three to our amigos so we chatted her up and invited her to lunch."

"We've been a trio ever since," Devon smiled.

Entrees were served and Symone wished she could put it in a doggy bag and head home. Instead, she bowed her head and blessed the food.

"You said grace already," Tanesha said.

"That was for the appetizers," Symone said. "This is a totally different meal."

"So you say grace every time something new is brought to the table?" Devon asked.

Symone placed a piece of salmon in her mouth and nodded. "Different hands could've prepared the food so I bless everything."

"Let me get you to bless my drinks then," Clinton joked. "Tell *Gawd* to keep the streets clear of cops when I drive home tonight."

Regina slid her hand under the table and gently squeezed Symone's thigh. Symone fought the urge to reply with a sarcastic comment for Regina's sake.

"And how are things between you two?" Anita inquired like a psychologist during a therapy session.

"Excuse me?" Symone responded with obvious agitation.

"Oh, don't be shy," Clinton cut in. "We're all family here."

"I don't know ya'll."

"Symone—" Regina warned as she inconspicuously grabbed the salad fork from the side of her plate and placed it in her lap.

"What?" Symone said. "She should know better."

Regina jabbed Symone in the leg with the fork then addressed the table. "What she means is that we don't talk about our personal lives."

"Don't matter how you spin it, Reggie. She was out of line for asking that question in the first place."

"I'm with you, Symone," Devon said, breaking the tension. "The best way to keep people out of your business is to keep your business to yourself and that's doubly true for a pro athlete." Devon nudged Anita playfully. "Girl, you know that."

"How 'bout we move on to something more relevant," Clinton stated. He turned to Symone and asked, "What causes are you looking forward to tackling?"

Symone looked at him confused. "Causes?"

"Sure. Right now the big ticket is discrimination." He turned and addressed the table, "Did you see that HB 1515 fell one vote short in passing."

"Did *you* hear what one of the members said in why they voted against it?" Tanesha informed, "He said he believes homosexuality is wrong so he couldn't support the bill."

"What?" Anita said shocked.

"I told you, we need to be more vocal in demanding our rights," Clinton said. "And having you, Symone, is a big plus."

"I'm still not understanding what I have to do with anything."

"You're an *out* professional athlete," Tanesha chimed in. "You standing up for a cause could be huge in—"

"I'm not trying to be a gay rights activist. I just wanna play ball."

Clinton was taken back by the abrupt statement.

"The gay and lesbian community is growing here in Charlotte, especially within the African American community." Tanesha looked Symone square in the eyes and stated firmly, "Your presence and support can really make a difference."

"Think about you and Regina," Devon interjected. "I'm sure you'd like to get married one day but gay marriage is not recognized. Even if you had a ceremony, legally, your commitment to each other means nothing."

Symone hesitated to respond to their remarks. She never thought about how being in the public's eye could make her a poster child to progress the movement for gay rights. She wasn't even sure if she was ready to accept that responsibility at only 22 years old.

"We're taking a little bit of time to get settled her in Charlotte first," Regina answered in Symone's silence.

"Give her the opportunity to have a fabulous rookie year and use that success to grab the ears of many."

"I like it," Clinton said like a giddy two year old. "Give her time to grow as a brand then use the name to change the game. Heyyy!"

"Already sounding like a First Lady," Anita said, grinning at Regina.

SYMONE EXHALED SLOWLY AS she rested in the driver's seat of the car. "That was bru-tal."

Regina sat in the passenger side with her arms folded across her chest. "I am *not* talking to you."

"What I do?"

"I know you're seriously not asking me that question."

"Reggie, they're nothing but a bunch of catty, shallow women, Clinton included." Regina gasped, upset with Symone's judgment of her friends. "Don't look at me like that," Symone carried on, "They said it themselves. They only became friends with you because you gotta nice body. And what was with all the valley girl talk." Symone flicked her wrists and mocked, "Oh my god, Reggie is such a cute nickname. We've been a trio ever since." Symone rolled her eyes. "I thought I was watching *Clueless* or something."

"So now you're judging them because they sound like rich and spoiled 'white girls'."

"Oh, this has nothing to do with race. I can't stand nobody who talk like that. White, black, Latina, Asian—I don't think I've ever heard an Asian talk like that though."

Regina waved her hand to bring Symone back to the conversation. "Regardless, you were out of line."

"No, I did good. You should be *very* proud of me. I could've called your boy Clinton out when he asked the waiter to move the chair and plates when he could've did it himself. And then got the nerve to ask me to move?"

Symone turned to Regina and asked sternly, "And what was the whole, 'you always *let me* have the end'. I sit where I good and well please."

"Whatever, Symone."

"And while we're talking about seating arrangements, your girl Zen ain't slick either. She wanted to sit across from you for a reason."

"She's my friend, Symone."

"Yeah. A real flirty friend." Symone continued with her over exaggerated impersonations. "Ooo, Regina, you're sooo gorgeous. I never seen you with your hair up. Can I suck on your neck like a vampire?"

Regina laughed to herself. "I don't know why I expected you to act civilized out in public. You've never been any good with that."

"Okay, fine. Let's not talk about me. Sam's been to visit, right? She met them? What she say?" Regina swept the strands of hair from her forehead and didn't answer. "Exactly!" Symone stated emphatically.

"Look I know they can be a bit abrasive—"

"And stuck up and shallow—"

"Okay, I said. Either way, they're still my friends and you embarrassed me tonight."

Regina turned her back to Symone and stared out the window.

"You should've warned me and let me know what I was walking into ahead of time." When Regina didn't respond, Symone resumed, "Now I get the silent treatment. That's cool. I'll give you the silent treatment for putting me through that."

Symone drove for less than a block before asking in a charming voice, "You still love me?" Regina just shifted her weight to keep Symone from seeing the smile trying to force itself upon her face. "You know you still love me," Symone stated with a smile. Symone kept picking with Regina until she started laughing.

"Ooo! I can't stand you sometimes," Regina smacked Symone playfully on the arm.

"But you still love me."

Regina playfully rolled her eyes, "I guess."

"Um hmm, keep playing *First Lady.*"

Chapter 13

"Three things will last forever—faith, hope and
love—and the greatest of these is love."
~ 1 Corinthians 13:13

THE WARM CHARLOTTE NIGHT did not come with
a refreshing cool breeze like the nights in Norfolk but it
was still comfortable. Symone held her arms out to her
sides as the bouncer patted the sides of her maroon and
gold striped long-sleeved shirt and the pockets of her
relaxed fit blue jeans. Symone took comfort in the fact
that her face had not become familiar among the locals
yet. She knew it would only be a matter of time before
she wouldn't be able to walk the streets by herself.

Symone scanned the bar and noticed a few of the
players near the pool tables close to the rear exit.

"Look who finally decided to come out?" Taneah
said.

Symone gave a half smile and exchanged
pleasantries with the group. "Yeah, well I figured if I kept
ditching you guys you might not pass me the ball when
the season begins."

"Shit, if you can come into the league and average
twenty plus right off the bat, I'll let you ditch us any time
you want," Alex, a veteran player said.

Symone smiled when she saw Candace joined the
group a few minutes after her.

"You finally accepted the invite," Candace said as she hugged Symone.

Symone wasn't sure why but she hoped her cologne wasn't too overpowering for Candace's liking.

"Yeah, I thought it was about time I stopped being antisocial." Symone gave Candace the once over and joked, "I see you're trying to dress like me."

Candace was casually dressed in denim skinny jeans, a light gray scoop neck shirt and denim jacket.

"No," she stated, "I think you peeked into *my* closet before getting dressed."

Symone smiled but decided to end the banter when she noticed a few of the players watching them. She surveyed the environment and nodded in approval. "This is a nice place."

"This is one of the most popular spots in Charlotte," Helen said. "And it's a mixed crowd so you're bound to meet a lot of interesting people."

"What's up with the name Dizzies?" Symone asked about the name of the bar. "Do I need to stay away from some specialty drink or something?"

"It's named after the owner's boyfriend," Helen answered.

"Oh, so a gay couple owns this."

"Kinda." Symone looked confused so Helen explained, "The owner was married and he was celebrating his birthday with some friends. They told him they were taking him to a strip club but they played a joke on him and took him to a drag show instead."

"He still claims he never knew it was a man on stage because he never knew a man could shake it like that," Candace added.

Gia laughed at her thought then exclaimed, "And that the belly dancing hypnotized him and that's how he fell in love with a man."

"I still say he had a little sugar in his tank to begin with," Alex said.

"Here we go—" Candace said rolling her eyes.

"Can you really tell me that if someone is straight and has no interest or attraction at all to the opposite sex, seeing a man dressed in drag is going to suddenly spark something that's gonna have him leave his wife of twelve years? I don't believe it."

"That's why I don't hang around a lot of gay people," Alex said. "No offense Symone but if the owner can turn that quick—"

"Hanging around gay people isn't gonna make you gay." Symone rolled her eyes at the thought. She tried to remain cordial since she didn't know the team well and she didn't want to come across as difficult. "You may be right. He might've been closeted or might've even been ashamed to admit it to himself. Sometimes you don't know until you meet someone who fall in love with at first sight." Symone found herself rambling the thoughts flowing through her head. "And why do people think homosexuality is contagious and?"

"I know right. It's not like the flu where if they cough on you, you've caught lesbianism."

"Yeah, it's a choice."

"Being gay is not a choice."

Alex saw Symone was getting annoyed and didn't want to argue so simply responded with, "Okay."

"Do you really think the owner *chose* to leave his wife after twelve years of marriage just to be with a man?"

"Maybe he and his wife were going through something and he used it as an excuse to get out the marriage."

Symone hated defending who she was to people, especially those who didn't know her but she was tired of people thinking it's easy to come to terms with one's sexuality. She was tired of people thinking it's easy to live one's life as a homosexual.

******

IT WAS A COOL brisk Friday evening in March and Symone was happy that the weekend had finally arrived. Classes were becoming harder but not because of the work. Sophomore year of high school seemed to be easier than her freshman year. Symone was making A's without even breaking a sweat but love was another story. Symone never found herself attracted to anyone, male or female for a long time. Until now, basketball and softball were the only two things she loved but the emergence of Kidera Fuentes changed all that and now Symone could not figure out why she felt so strongly toward this Puerto Rican beauty.

Symone knew she had romantic feelings for Kidera but she didn't understand how. Her parents never talked about homosexuality but she knew from church sermons that being with someone of the same sex was a sin. She'd been trying so hard to live a good life since her grandmother passed away so how could this be something she would be dealing with? Was God punishing her for something? Was she paying for the sins of someone else in the family? Maybe this was a generational curse that's been passed down and now it was on her. All these thoughts swarmed Symone's mind everyday but seeing Kidera in homeroom every morning warmed her insides like hot cocoa on a cold winter night. She couldn't stop thinking about her even when she was home. Symone's outlet in shooting free throws to clear her thoughts was no help either since Kidera's older sister Kyra played on the basketball team also. There was no escape from these feelings and Symone cried herself to sleep every night not knowing of what to do.

In Psychology class earlier that day, Symone was paired with Kidera to do a project on homelessness in America. Neither one of them were able to make eye contact with each other as they sketched out a rough draft for their project in class and exchanged numbers to meet sometime during the weekend after doing individual research. Symone was excited and scared about her pending meet with Kidera on Saturday and the tension weighing on her shoulders caused her neck to stiffen.

It was the evening of her mother's thirty-eighth birthday and after dinner and cake with her parents, Symone decided to go in the backyard and hit a few softballs. She really wanted to talk to someone about what she was feeling for Kidera but who could she tell? Definitely not her parents or her brother. She didn't have money to pay a psychiatrist. She thought about the pastor but he was the one who preached homosexuality was wrong. She knew she could always go to God with everything for He knew all anyway but was she ready to call herself a homosexual? Was she truly ready to accept that she was a lesbian? The bible says, what a man thinks in his heart, so is he. If she believed these feelings were real and spoke them aloud, would the universe follow her lead and establish her words in stone? The thought of disappointing her parents and more importantly, God overwhelmed Symone. She tossed a softball in the air and swung at it with all her might. The metal bat connecting with the oversized ball stung her chilled, ungloved hands. Night had settled and Symone could not see where the ball landed to retrieve it.

"Great," she said aloud. "Hitting something actually feels good but I don't know where the stupid ball is to work out the rest of this aggression."

Symone paced the backyard, thinking of a new plan. She stared at the huge oak tree standing tall in the middle of the backyard. She looked down at the bat and knew if hitting the ball stung her hands, swinging the bat at the tree may very well cause her whole body to chime. Symone glanced around and saw huge trunks of timber her father used for firewood. She could have a better chance swinging the lumber but it was too thick around to hold. Symone suddenly remembered that she has a wood bat she practiced with in the off-season. She fumbled around in the backyard and found it lying next to the clothesline.

The bat was pretty thick and Symone wondered how many swings she could get out of it before it broke against the solid bark of the oak tree. She assumed three. Symone sized up the tree and took one strong swing at the tree. Releasing the pent up energy inside her felt better than she expected. She took a deep breath and sized the tree up again. Crack!

Symone lied on the ground with the right side of her head throbbing. She wasn't sure of what happened until the tears pouring from her right eye slowed enough for her to see. The head of the bat broke, ricocheted off the tree and hit her square in the face. Symone's hands shook as she used her shirt to dry her face. That was when she saw the blood.

It didn't take long for her mother's panic attack to begin when she saw Symone stagger into the living room with a gash over her right eye, blood spilling down her face.

"Oh my god!" Paula jumped off the sofa and inspected Symone's wound. "What happened?"

"I hit myself in the face with the bat," Symone stated plainly.

"How—" Paula disregarded asking the question. Her children were known for testing their mortality but this was the first time they would end up in the emergency room because of it.

****

"SO WAIT—" TANEAH WANTED to make sure she understood Symone's story, "you split your eye open over a girl?"

Symone nodded. "Gave myself a concussion too. And mind you, this was before anything ever happened with Kid. I nearly knocked myself out because of the convictions I had about loving this girl way *before* I even tried to express that love to her." She turned to Alex and asked, "If being gay was really a choice, why did it hurt so much to love her? Why didn't I just choose someone else, a guy for that matter?"

"Okay, I can kinda see where you're coming from with that but they're too many gays and lesbians that fall in and out of love so quick—"

"Some may've never really felt love," Candace spoke up. "It's just like someone who comes from an abusive home. Someone shows you a little attention and you fall in love with how they make you feel because there's no pain associated with it."

"Love is like an addiction."

Members of the group nodded in agreement.

"Love is definitely a drug—"

"And you'll go through the same highs and lows if it's not shared with the right person."

"I just think if he still loved his wife, he wouldn't have left like that after twelve years."

Symone shrugged her shoulders. "I never said love made sense but when it comes to love, there's no such thing as having a choice."

Chapter 14

"Owe nothing to anyone—except for your
obligation to love one another." ~ Romans 13:8

SYMONE CHECKED THE TIME and saw she had
thirty minutes until Regina came home from work. All of
Symone's ingredients were prepped and now she was
ready to start cooking. Symone checked the temperature
of the steamer then added the broccoli. The water boiled
on the back burner so Symone poured in the box of
butterfly pasta noodles. She placed a few drops of oil on
the stovetop grill then lined the grill with the shrimp
kabobs.

"Oh yeah." Symone wiped her hands on her
apron. "Those chefs on the Food Network and Cooking
Channel better watch out now!" She picked up a cut
lemon and lime and squeezed the juices over the kabobs.
The grill sizzled in delight. Symone licked the juices off
her fingers and said proudly, "I might have to switch
professions once I'm finish playing basketball."

The last few weeks had been a roller coaster ride
and Symone wanted to bring the love back into her
relationship with Regina. Her plan was to make the
evening all about Regina because she knew the
circumstances looming in Virginia would soon become a
priority, changing both their lives.

Symone heard the key enter the lock of the front door just as she poured sauce over the plate.

"Perfect timing," Symone smiled in satisfaction. "Hey baby," Symone greeted as she wiped her hands on the dishtowel.

"Hey," Regina dragged. "Something smells good."

"I cooked dinner."

Regina looked at Symone suspiciously as she took off her blazer. "What you do?"

Symone smacked her lips. "Why you think I did something?"

"Because you don't cook dinner." Symone gave Regina the side eye so Regina clarified, "You haven't cooked dinner lately."

"Which is why I did it." Symone walked over and kissed Regina on the cheek. "Come sit down with me while the food cools off."

Regina's eyes narrowed as she followed Symone to the sofa. Symone reached for Regina's feet and slipped off her heels. She draped Regina's leg across her lap and massaged her feet.

"Now I know you did something because you've never massaged my feet."

Symone grinned. "I'm not really a feet person am I?"

"No, you're not."

"Honestly Reggie, I just—I just wanted us to take a night and focus on us."

"Is this about dinner with my friends?"

"No woman! It's about us. I've been here for less than a month and we've argued more than our entire relationship. I just wanted to do something to get us back where we used to be."

Regina still felt there was more to the story but she decided not to push the issue. Symone was right. Their relationship had been a bit rocky since Symone graduating from college and making the permanent move to Charlotte. Whatever the reason, Regina hoped to enjoy the evening loving her girlfriend.

After dinner, Symone and Regina cuddled on the sofa eating Tiramisu while listening to their autographed album from Kenny G.

"Remember in college when you had Kenny G come out to the beach and play for me?"

"Of course I do. I had to pull a lot of strings to make that happen."

"You never told me you knew Kenny G."

"That's because I don't," Symone laughed. "The calligraphy business I owned, one of my clients knew Kenny G and I used to talk about how much I loved his music. The client told me that Kenny G was in North Carolina that weekend doing a concert so I asked for a favor."

"A pretty huge favor, I bet."

"Oh yeah. Let's just say I had to do a number of invitations pro bono but it was worth it."

"Do you ever wish you kept the business? I know how much you love to do calligraphy."

"I can still do it but it was too much to handle, the business side of it with basketball, softball and school. High school classes were so easy for me but college, man, holding a 3.0 GPA was harder than I thought it would be. Besides, the money I got from selling the business is growing into a nice little nest egg for us."

"Oh is it?"

"Yeah, you know. For when we start talking about getting married and having kids and stuff."

Regina hid her smile as she looked up at Symone. "And when are we going to start talking about that."

Symone knew Regina was trying to bait her into the 'what does our future hold' conversation but Symone wasn't ready to budge.

"How 'bout a year from now."

"A year?"

"Yeah. that'll give me one solid year in the league and you'll be doing your thing at the magazine. We can talk then and see if you're ready to neglect that perfect body of yours to some stretch marks."

"Who said I was having the babies?"

Symone gave Regina the side eye but postponed her comment to answer her cell phone.

"Hello?"

"Hey dad."

Regina shifted her weight so Symone could get up from the sofa. Symone took her phone conversation into the bedroom. Regina sighed heavily and made her way to the kitchen to clean up the dishes. She didn't like it when Symone isolated herself when it came to her family but tonight was not the night to bring it up. Symone worked so hard to give them some much needed quality time and Regina didn't want to ruin it by arguing with her about her family.

"Everything okay?" Regina asked when Symone came back into the front of the house.

"Not really but I don't want to talk about it tonight."

"You sure?"

"Yeah." Symone walked over and took the dishes from Regina's hands. "Leave these til morning."

"Symone, you know I don't like to—"

Symone kissed Regina passionately on the mouth to stop her from talking. "Come lay with me."

Regina saw the hurt and worry in Symone's eyes. Her heart softened and she vowed to do everything within her power to take Symone's pain away. Even if it was only for that night.

Chapter 15

"Love never gives up, never loses faith, is always hopeful, and endures through every circumstance." ~ 1 Corinthians 13:7

THE RINGING OF THE doorbell jarred Symone from her sleep. She struggled to lift her head as the comforter enveloped her in darkness.

"Reggie." Her coarse voice barely reached above a whisper. When the chiming stopped, Symone assumed the unwelcomed visitor gave up and moved on.

Before Regina spoke a single word, Symone knew she had reentered the bedroom. The scent of *Hypnose* perfume by *Lancôme* tickled Symone's nostrils and brought a smile to her face just like the coffee commercials she admired on television. Symone wasn't sure of the time but after the previous night's sexcapade, she hoped Regina planned to hop back into bed for a quick encore before leaving for work.

"Symone?"

Regina's tone was that of curiosity and confusion, nothing close to the sensual purring Symone expected.

"Yeah," Symone mumbled from under the covers.

"UPS just dropped off a package from your Aunt Betty."

Symone emerged from under the plush comforter and stared quizzically at the brown box. "Is it a book?" she guessed by the rectangular shape.

Regina didn't answer. Symone knew she hadn't opened the box so Regina refused to entertain the question by answering with the obvious.

Symone reluctantly rolled to the edge of the bed and retrieved the box from Regina. She grabbed Regina's hand and pulled her gently to the bed. Regina fell into Symone's embrace and giggled like a school girl as Symone placed wet kisses on the back of her neck.

"How much time you got?" Symone asked seductively.

"Hmm, no time unfortunately."

"How you got NO time?"

"I overslept because of you."

Symone's immediate silence made Regina curious. She looked back and found Symone grinning in satisfaction. Regina couldn't help but laugh.

"You're too much."

"And you know that's right!"

Regina kissed Symone on the lips and stood to her feet. She checked her white stretch dress pants for lint before stepping into her pink lemonade-colored open toe heels.

"I have to go, baby." Regina leaned forward and planted another kiss on Symone's lips.

Symone rubbed Regina's bare arms and felt the goose bumps.

"Before you say anything," Regina began her defense, "my jacket's already out front *and* it matches my shoes."

"I'm not worried about you getting chilly but those sexy arms may give someone else the wrong kind of chills."

Regina rolled her eyes and pointed to the box. "Why don't you see what your Aunt sent you and stop worrying about Zen."

Symone rolled her eyes playfully as she pulled the tab on the box. The contents that fell out left them both speechless.

"Is that—"

"Yeah."

Regina moved slowly back to the bed and sat down gingerly next to Symone. In Symone's hands was a two-inch three-ring binder with a picture of her grandmother on the front cover jacket. Symone opened the binder and found a card from her Aunt in the front pocket.

Symone,

One of my dearest friends put this binder together of all the articles my sister, your grandmother wrote over the years for The Perquimans Weekly. She mentioned you in a few of her articles. I wanted to share her works with you and give you the opportunity to read for yourself the kind of person your grandmother really was. I still miss her but God's will must be done.

Love,
Aunt Betty

Regina wiped the tears from her eyes then kissed those that fell from Symone's.

"I'll let you have some time alone," Regina said softly. "I'll see you when I get home."

Symone stared at the binder and exhaled loudly. "Aunt Betty, Aunt Betty."

Symone rustled her hair with both hands, waking it up. Her stomach reminded her she had not eaten in close to ten hours but Symone couldn't tear her eyes away from the binder. She flipped through it liberally until she found an article that caught her attention.

"Children Need Positive Self-Concept," Symone read the title aloud.

She began reading the article to herself and a third of the way in, she received the validation she had been searching for her entire life.

> *"To grow up happy, every child needs to feel loved, to be held and played with, to know that his parents love, want, and enjoy him, to know that what happens to him matters to someone. A child needs to feel accepted, and that his parents like him for himself, just the way he is. He also needs to know that they like him all the time and not only when he acts according to their idea of the way a child should act. He should know that they always accept him, even though they may not approve of the things he does, that they will let him grow and develop in his own way."*

Symone moved the binder from her lap to the bed. She sat quietly and allowed her grandmother's words to resonate within her spirit.

A flood of thoughts washed through Symone's mind. *Did grandma know I was gay? How did she find out? Was she trying to let me know it was okay, that she was okay with it?* Symone suddenly remembered something and immediately scurried to the bedroom closet. All the way in the back stuffed in the bottom of a duffle bag was a shoebox for toddler shoes. Symone hid the tiny box, covering it with loose-leaf papers and an assortment of fitted skullcaps. She and Regina made a deal that when they moved in together, they would not bring old love letters or any personal items from previous relationships into the house. If they wanted to keep the mementos, they had to go in storage. Symone did not have a problem putting old gifts away in storage but the letters from Kidera were harder for her to let go of mainly because they were written during the time Symone and her mother's relationship started to deteriorate. They were not love letters, but letters of assurance that everything would end up all right. Symone never explained this to Regina. She assumed anything from Kidera was off limits and not allowed in the house. Symone hated breaking her promise to Regina but the conversation she had with her dad the night before was the exact reason why she needed those letters close by.

Symone skimmed many of the letters and smiled at the comfort they still brought her after all these years. As she sifted through the correspondence, separating supporting emails from happy birthday cards, Symone found what she was looking for. Staring back at her was the letter she wrote her grandmother in 1997, a year after she passed away. There were many things Symone felt she never got to say or ask her grandmother and too many questions went unanswered. Symone felt guilty for not spending more time with her during her second bout of cancer so she wrote the letter hoping to release some of the hurt and guilt that plagued her most of her freshman year of high school.

Symone carefully placed the letter on the floor next to her and stuffed the other materials back into the shoebox. She sat on the floor against the bed with her knees pulled into her chest and stared at the letter for what seemed like an eternity. Symone debated on whether she wanted to read it or not. She knew the contents of the letter would unleash a flood of emotions she was not sure she wanted to set free. Masking her pain was how she survived the last nine years or maybe it was the reason she had not completely healed yet.

"You just had to start it didn't you, Aunt Betty." Symone let out an extended verbal sigh. "Well, if I'm gonna face it, might as well face it all," she said as she unfolded the worn, but well-preserved paper.

Today marks the one-year anniversary of your homegoing. I was only 13 years old when you passed away. It was a huge shock to my system even though it shouldn't have been. This was your second bout with cancer and you weren't doing as good as the first time around. We all were expecting the worse but I didn't believe God would take you away because He knew I still needed you. He had to know, especially now with all these feelings I have for this new girl in my school. Aunt Betty always tells me I'm so much like you but I never knew what you were like when you were my age. Did you always feel alone too? Like, you didn't fit in anywhere? I wish I knew. If you did, I'd feel so much better because then I'd know I was going to turn out okay. But this thing with liking girls has really got my head all messed up, grandma. I wish I could talk to you, ask you what you think about it. I know mom and dad are gonna flip out and it hurts me thinking that this will hurt them so much but I just don't know what to do. I can't pretend to like guys. THAT would be wrong, right? I don't wanna get married someday and be stuck in a loveless marriage just to make everyone else feel better. My life should be about me being happy, not anybody else. I've prayed over and over for God to take this feeling out of me if this isn't who He wants me to be. I don't wanna make Him mad at me too. Why did He have to take you away from me before I got a chance to learn more about myself through you? All the summers me and Ant used to spend at your house for vacation bible school. Then I got into basketball which turned into summer league games. I traded learning about my future, my life for a game and now none of it seems important anymore. I'm just going through the motions with basketball, playing because quitting, well, that's just not in me either. I wonder if this is how Michael Jordan felt after his dad was killed? Maybe I should do like he did and just take some time off to deal with you not being here anymore. I never really mourned you, ya know. I just pretend you're at your house in North Carolina and that's why I don't see you. Maybe God knew best though. He knew how much I looked up to you and if you would've told me you weren't happy with me liking girls, I would've been crushed. Not having your love would've made me want to kill myself or live a lie by locking these feelings away forever.

"You're the only one I would've changed my life for," Symone read aloud, her vision blurred by her tears.

"I would've given anything to have one more night with you. One more conversation, one more hug, one more smile, one more goodbye."

Symone closed her eyes and sobbed like a sick infant.

"Thank you, God." She turned and knelt before the binder on the bed. "Thank you so much for this."

It was the first time Symone truly felt at peace with her sexual identity. The weight of her childhood struggles lifted off her chest. She could breathe easy now heading into a bright future.

Symone stuffed the letter inside the paper protector at the end of the binder. She still felt she chose basketball over learning more about her grandmother, learning more about herself. She did not want that guilt to fester inside her any longer.

SYMONE WALKED ACROSS THE gymnasium floor with a lot more confidence in her step. The decision she made was hard but necessary. Not too many people got the chance to right past wrongs. Symone had a second chance at putting family first. She wasn't about to let her opportunity pass her by again.

Symone stood in the doorway of the training room and knocked on the peeling doorframe.

Candace looked up from her computer and smiled. "Hey Symone."

"Hey. You busy?"

"Just surfing the net." Candace stopped typing and smiled, "It's the Friday before your first pro game. You nervous yet?"

"It's just a preseason game," Symone said nonchalantly, her hands stuffed deep into her jean pockets.

"But it's your pro debut."

"Well, maybe not."

Candace looked at Symone confused. "Are you injured? Do you need treatment? I didn't see you at practice earlier today."

"Yeah, um, I met with coach and some of the front office staff."

"Is everything okay?"

Symone rubbed the back of her neck then answered, "I'm leaving for a while. Taking the season off actually."

Candace was surprised by the news. She walked over to Symone and asked, "What happened?"

"I need to go back to Virginia. Help out with my mom, ya know."

"Sure, of course. I understand." Candace paused for a moment then said, "You're leaving before Sunday's game?"

"I thought about waiting until after the game but I know me. Playing pro ball is all I ever wanted to do. If I go up to Connecticut—"

"Like you said, it's just the preseason."

"But it'll be my first experience as a pro player. Hearing the cheers or boos and if I prove to myself I really can match up and play with these women—I know for sure I wouldn't be able to make this decision to leave." Symone thought for a moment. "Yeah, I gotta go now before I know what—well, I know but before I *really* know what I'm giving up."

"That makes a lot of sense, Symone. I hope everything works out with your mom."

"Me too. Anyway, I didn't wanna leave without saying goodbye."

"I'm glad you didn't. Good luck with everything. We'll miss you 'round here."

"I'm not gone forever, ya know," Symone laughed.

"I know but—you know what I mean."

"Yeah I know. Well, I better get going."

"Stay in touch okay."

Symone only offered a sorrowful smile as she waved and headed for the exit.

Chapter 16

"I prayed to the LORD, and he answered me. He freed me from all my fears." ~ Psalms 34:4

SYMONE SAT AT THE computer and watched as Regina prepared for bed. The silk robe she wore hung loosely on her small but curvy frame. Regina had her hair tied up in a bun, exposing the nape of her neck as she took her earrings off and placed them on top of the dresser. Symone knew the next part of Regina's nighttime ritual would be her lathering her body with vanilla scented lotion. Symone wanted to sneak up behind her and kiss the spots on Regina's neck, shoulders and back that made her warm to postpone the inevitable argument she was not looking forward to starting. However, she knew she couldn't stall any longer. She had to tell Regina about the conversation she had with her father and her thoughts in response to it.

"Remember the call I took from my dad the other night?" Symone asked.

"Um hmm," Regina muttered without taking her eyes off her refection in the mirror.

"His insurance request was denied. He's not gonna get the help he needs to take care of my mom."

Regina finally turned and faced Symone. "Honey, I'm so sorry."

"Yeah."

"What's he going to do? Does he know?"

"He says he's gonna take care of her himself. The insurance won't pay for a physical therapist and he doesn't have money to pay for one so he's gonna do it."

Regina was touched by Symone's father's chivalrous act. Regina's father left her mother and she resented him for breaking both their hearts and tearing their family apart. "He's doing what a man is supposed to do. I wish my dad loved my mom like that."

"Yeah, but he don't know nothing about training and fitness. His intent is good but he might do more harm than good."

"Maybe you should get with Antoine and see if he can help."

"I called Ant but he got two kids with one on the way. Trying to get momma back where she needs to be will be too much for him too."

"What about writing up a training plan for your dad? Give him a guide to follow. Maybe offer to pay for a physical therapist to work with her or call Chief or Kyra—"

"It's not their job to take care of *my* mother!" Symone shouted.

"You just said your dad doesn't know what he's doing," Regina fired back in a raised voice. She closed her eyes and took a deep breath. "You have to use the people around you, Symone. That's why they're there. They're your army or do you feel they're not strong enough either."

Regina knew the statement was a low blow but Symone needed to hear it.

Symone gave her an apathetic look and pleaded, "Can we not get into that right now?"

"Fine but what else can you do to help him?"

Symone knew the time had come. There was no easy way to say it so she sucked in a deep breath and stated firmly, "I've decided to take the year off from playing ball to move back home and help my dad get my mom back to where she needs to be."

The words came out so unexpectedly, Regina had to sit down and allow them to soak in. After processing the information, Regina still couldn't believe the decision Symone made without talking to her about it first.

"You what?"

"I gotta go home, Reggie."

"And when were you going to tell me this?"

"I'm telling you now." The number of emotions that rose inside Regina ranged from hurt to anger to disappointment, all of which Symone saw in her face. "Look, I only made the decision yesterday. It's not like I've been holding out on you. I wanted to pray on it first. Figure out if this was the right thing to do."

"I—how—when—" too many questions flooded Regina's mind as she tried to make sense of what was going on.

Symone moved to the bed and sat down next to her. She took Regina's hands in hers and looked her straight in her eyes.

"I know you think I have other options but I don't. Ant can only do so much and you know how he and my dad be bumping heads. And with Chief and Kyra, do you really think my mom's gonna let one of them in the house let alone help her?" Regina hated to admit it but Symone had a point. "Paying someone to work with her could be good but she's stubborn. I want someone who knows her and will push her to get back where she needs to be. I just think this is the best way and it may be God's way of giving me and my mom another chance at fixing our relationship."

There weren't too many times Regina and Symone saw eye to eye about anything let alone plans that dealt with her family. Regina always felt left out of the loop but she actually agreed with Symone this time. Maybe God allowed this tragedy to happen so Symone and her mother would have an opportunity to repair what was broken years ago. Who was she to stand in the way of that?

"Okay," Regina finally spoke up.

Symone looked at her shocked. "What?"

"I said okay. Maybe this is your chance to heal the wounds that are still open in your heart. If going back to Virginia will do that—then okay."

Symone was so overwhelmed with joy. She never expected Regina to be so understanding but Regina's next statement explained why.

"I'll talk to Rosalyn tomorrow and see if I can take emergency leave or at least use the rest of my vacation days—"

Regina's voice became a blur as Symone closed her eyes and inhaled deeply.

"I'm going alone, Reggie," Symone blurted out over her rambling. The heavy panting was Symone's first indicator that Regina's anger had resurfaced. "Before you snap, just listen, okay. I haven't talked to my dad or Ant yet about this."

Regina's expression changed immediately. "Why haven't you talked with them?"

"Well one, I wanted to make sure I could take the year off from the league and two, I wanted to talk with you about it first." Regina's demeanor softened. "I know you think I don't include you in a lot of things I do but I think about how it's gonna affect you, Reggie. I wanted to make sure things would be good here before getting anyone's hopes up up there."

"So you already talked with the coach?"

"Yeah. My contract will be postponed due to a family emergency. As long as I come back to training camp next year in shape to play, everything in the contract will become valid then."

"Okay but I still don't see why I can't go with you?"

"I don't even know where I'm staying at when I get there, Reggie. Not to mention convincing my mom to train with me is gonna take some work. Showing up with you may make it impossible for her to accept my help."

"But—"

"I'm going off a whim, Reggie. Just give me a week or two after I get up there to figure things out. If Ant has the space, maybe we can stay with him. And this'll give you time to square things at your job instead of rushing off and jeopardizing all the hard work you've put in."

Regina could tell Symone had practiced this speech many times. She already had a response to every rebuttal Regina challenged her with.

"Okay," Regina gave in, "but after two weeks we're going to talk about me coming up there." Regina grasped both sides of Symone's face with her hands. "While you're there for your mom, let me be there for you."

Symone nodded and kissed Regina softly on the lips. "You know, I was wrong in what I said last week." Regina stared in confusion as Symone explained, "You're not a weak solider. You're nowhere near it."

Regina wanted to make sure Symone was not just saying this to make her feel better so she asked, "Why do you think that now?"

"I'm not an easy person to deal with. I know I'm stubborn and it takes a strong woman to deal with that. And, God knows I've been through a lot with my family and He knows that I don't have the strength to deal with them and carry a weak woman along in the fight. He would've never sent you to me if you weren't strong enough to handle it and I thank Him for that."

"It's about time you recognized that," Regina said smiling.

"Trust me, I do." Symone caressed the sides of Regina's face with both hands. "I couldn't do this without you, Reggie. I mean that."

Part Three

Chapter 17

"I love you, LORD; you are my strength." ~
Psalms 18:1

I WAS EXCITED FOR my sophomore year to begin. For one, my brother finally graduated and now I would be known as something other than Antoine's baby sister. The second and most important reason was I would be the starting point guard for the varsity basketball team. I worked my way into the starting line up last year when the previous starting point guard was ineligible the second part of the season due to bad grades. So yeah, I was very excited for my sophomore year to begin...was.

 Thinking back on it now, I had always been drawn to women. I remember my kindergarten teacher. She was a tall, black woman with a radiant smile. I was only five but I knew there was something about her that made me want to be near her. She was the only reason I would leave my mom to go to school. Of course, I didn't know what I was feeling back then. I can't even say that what I felt was romantic. I just knew I felt safe with her. Her smile was warm and inviting and that made her nice to me.

 As I grew older, I didn't look at boys or girls sexually. Basketball was my true love and softball was my girlfriend on the side. That's where my focus was, where I put all my energy. It wasn't until my sophomore year of high school that things changed.

****

SYMONE STRETCHED HER ARMS out to her side, lifted her head to the sky and closed her eyes. The warmth from the sun beamed against the side of her face. Symone drew a deep breath as the cool breeze from the bay's waters chilled the outer layer of her skin just enough to raise goose bumps on her bare forearms. Symone felt at peace when she sat down at the docks of Waterside and promised herself the house she would raise her family in would have its own Waterside easily accessible right in her backyard.

"You can't expect this place to give you all the answers," an old but familiar voice said.

Symone smiled inwardly. She missed hearing the accent of Kidera's native tongue when she spoke.

"I don't." With her eyes still closed, Symone carried on, "The peacefulness allows me to escape the problem momentarily and more often than not, that's the only answer I need at that time. Just getting away."

Symone finally opened her eyes when she felt the wooden bench shift due to the addition of Kidera's weight.

"I could always find you here," Kidera said. "Whether things were going right or wrong, this place— was your home—more than anywhere else."

Symone purposely did not look at Kidera as she sat next to her on the bench. There was something about her silky golden skin paired with her brown wavy hair and soft Spanish accent that never failed at producing butterflies in Symone's stomach. That same feeling swept over Symone the first time she laid eyes on Kidera six years earlier.

******

HOMEROOM WAS FILLED WITH *the same familiar faces from her freshman year of high school. Symone wished she could change her last name and be assigned to a different class so she could* start every morning hanging with her friends. Luckily, Symone had one person in the class she could stand to be around.

"Yo, Shay Shay." Symone and Shaniese did their secret handshake then Symone sat down in the seat to the right of her.

"How was your summer?" Shaniese asked.

"All basketball," Symone grinned wide.

"That's cool. I'm just glad we're not freshman anymore."

"It never bothered me."

"That's 'cause you're Ms. Basketball star," Shaniese said in a condescending tone.

"Don't hate the pla-ya, hate the game!"

Shaniese smacked her lips. "Since we talking about game—" she tore a sheet of paper from her notebook.

"Oh, you don't want none."

"Sounds like you're punking out," Shaniese said as she folded the paper into a tight triangle.

"Why would I punk out?" Symone asked slyly. "You haven't beat me in paper football yet."

Shaniese turned her desk toward Symone. "Let's go then."

Symone smiled and aligned her desk with Shaniese. Shaniese started play by flicking the paper football across the table with her fingers. It stopped on her side of the desk.

"You can't even get the ball out of your own side of the field," Symone laughed. "This is gonna be too easy."

As Symone and Shaniese played their game, a late arrival entered the classroom.

"Sorry I'm late, Mrs. Weston. My sister stopped to get something to eat."

"It's fine, Kidera. Just find a seat."

Symone watched as Kidera faced the class looking for an empty desk. Their eyes locked and Symone's stomach tightened. Kidera smiled at her, tucked her hair behind her right ear and moved toward her. Symone's heartbeat quickened when Kidera brushed up against her and sat down at the desk across from her.

Symone kept her eyes on Kidera who tried to pretend she didn't notice Symone gazing at her.

"Touchdown!" Shaniese yelled, snapping Symone from her trance.

"What? Wait? You can't have touchdown. I didn't get my turn."

"You timed out. I betcha next time you'll pay attention."

****

"SO, HOW YOU BEEN?" Symone asked staring out at the water.

"Why don't we just skip the small talk, bien?" Kidera said. "You were never really good at it."

Symone smiled and placed her hands in her jacket pockets. "I hate the fact that after all these years you still know me so well."

"Me too sometimes though I did expect you to visit sooner." Kidera paused and snapped her fingers in sarcasm. "Oh, that's right. You were punishing me for you losing Kyra as a friend too."

"I wasn't punishing you."

"What would you call it then?"

"Consequences from your actions maybe?" Symone stated with her own sting of sarcasm.

"Tu tienes unos cojones."

"I got some nerve?" Symone shouted. "You cheated on me!"

"I was losing your heart!" Kidera shouted back. "You might suck at talking about you feelings but I could see you falling in love with Regina the moment I stepped foot on that campus."

"I never would've cheated on you, Kid."

Kidera shoulders slouched and replied, "You already had." She sighed and carried on, "I wasn't going to sit around and wait until Christmas break for you to give me some lame excuse on why we can't be together anymore so I made it easy for you. I gave you an out, Sy and don't act like you didn't want it."

"Maybe I did and maybe I should've been more of a woman and let you go when I knew I had feelings for Regina but I didn't want to throw away what we had not knowing for sure. That was the first time you and I had *ever* been apart and I thought me liking Regina was more out of loneliness than anything. That's one of the reasons Reggie and I didn't start dating until the end of the school year. We'd been through too much for me to just—leave you, Kid."

"I know and that's why I gave you a reason to leave. You may not've liked the way I did it but I couldn't sit back and watch you fall out of love with me and in love with someone else."

"I'm sorry, Kid. I didn't know—I didn't think about how I was hurting you."

"All I ever wanted was for you to be happy, Symone. You'd been through too much to not have that."

"I'm getting there," Symone exhaled loudly. "It's taking some time but I'm getting there."

Chapter 18

"For though I am far away from you, my heart is with you. And I rejoice that you are living as you should and that your faith in Christ is strong." ~ Colossians 2:5

SYMONE LEANED AGAINST THE hood of her Infiniti QX4 and stared at the house where she grew up. The one-story single family home was not hard to miss from the street. It was the only house left on the block. The other developments had been bought out by the local hospital who wanted the land to build an administration building. Symone's father was the last man standing and it was going to take more than an unappealing offer to get him to move.

Symone immediately noticed yellow, orange and purple flowers planted in the homemade flowerbed along the base of the pale blue house. There was a wooden rocking chair sitting on the front porch next to a portable bar. Symone's father always had the hobby of collecting odd items he found at junkyards or on the curb. Another man's trash was Frederick's treasure and his craftiness turned most of those treasures into valuable pieces of art.

Symone pushed herself off the SUV and stretched. "Can't turn back now," she said to herself as she mustered the courage to enter.

Frederick informed Symone when she called that he and her mom were out visiting a friend but he left the door unlocked for her. Symone found it fitting that she would walk through the front door and travel back in time alone.

****

SYMONE FELT SOMETHING WASN'T right before she even made it to the room where her grandmother rested. The family just returned from church where most either prayed for peace or a miracle in coping with the elderly woman's fading health.

The hospice nurse looked up from the book she was reading when Symone peeked her head inside the bedroom.

"You can come in," the hospice nurse said.

The thirteen-year-old Symone crept into the room gingerly and closed the door behind her. "How she doing?"

"The same."

Symone read between the lines. 'The same' was a euphemism for 'the end is near' but no one wanted to pass on the bad news of a loved one dying, especially to a child.

Symone had a softball game later that afternoon and she had been debating for days on whether she should go or not. She knew her grandmother did not want her to stop living her life on her account. Still, Symone was hesitant to leave, feeling as though she was choosing sports over her family.

Symone moved slowly to the bed and gazed at her grandmother. Her skin was pallid and wilted due to the chemotherapy stealing her appetite and draining her of what little nourishment the IV pumped through her bloodstream.

Symone leaned over her grandmother's brittle body and kissed her chalky forehead. "I'm heading to my game now, grandma," Symone spoke softly. "I'll be back to check on you later."

Her grandmother didn't respond. She just continued to lay with her eyes closed, breathing sparingly.

Symone walked toward the door when she heard the hospice nurse say, "Mrs. Frye, your granddaughter is leaving."

Symone turned around in time to see her grandmother open her eyes. She sat up and with what seemed to be her last breath, her grandmother said, "Goodbye Symone."

Tears weld up in Symone's eyes as her grandmother's body sunk back down and returned to its comatose state.

****

TEARS TRICKLED DOWN SYMONE'S cheeks as she rested her head against the bedroom doorpost where her grandmother passed away eight years ago. Even though the hospital bed had been replaced with a daybed and the walls was now a neutral canary yellow, the memories from that day still haunted her like overcast fog on a dark, dreary night.

"Symone?" Symone jumped at the sound of her father's voice. "Didn't mean to scare you. I thought you might've heard me come in."

"Nah, I didn't," Symone replied as she wiped her tears with the palms of her hands. "I was—someplace else." Symone looked up into her dad's weary brown eyes and said, "Ya know, I knew she was gone before you came back to the field to pick me up. I just—the air around me felt different while I was in the dugout. There was this—cloud of sadness I couldn't shake. Then I saw you and it all made sense. I knew."

"They say you can feel when someone close to you dies."

"*I* knew she was gonna leave us that day as soon as she said goodbye to me. I never should've left, I never should've left."

"She wasn't alone. Aunt Carol was in there with her."

"Still—"

Without warning, Symone's shoulders tensed up at the sound of her mother's electric scooter coasting toward them.

"What's she doing here?" her mother asked, noticeably agitated by Symone's presence.

"Paula, I told you she's going to——"

"I told you to tell her not to come."

"Well, I didn't."

Paula glared at Frederick with disdain. Still not acknowledging Symone, she pushed the joystick on the electric scooter and motored passed them to the master bedroom at the end of the hallway.

Symone spoke up before her father had a chance to justify her mother's actions. "It's okay, dad. Don't worry about it."

"I know you're okay."

Symone smiled and glanced back into the front bedroom. She still had not crossed the threshold to enter. The house had become a time capsule and each room catapulted her back to an event she wished she could forget.

"But about me staying here——"

"I already talked to Antoine to see if he had space at his house," Frederick said. "I figured it might be—well, hard to sleep here."

Relief swept over Symone's body, removing the burden of her having to be strong before she was ready.

"Thanks."

"Have you figured out how you're going to get your mother to work with you?"

"Nope but I'm sure God will give me a plan soon or at least I hope he will."

Chapter 19

"The father instantly cried out, 'I do believe, but help me overcome my unbelief.'" ~ Mark 9:24

SYMONE CLOSED HER EYES and drew in a deep breath as she stood outside the doors of Faith in God's Love Ministries. She attended a number of churches since leaving Virginia but none was like her home church led by Bishop Elliott Reed. There was something about his style of preaching that helped Symone understand the bible better. Bishop Reed didn't hoop and holler or perform any other types of theatrics to fool people into thinking they felt the Holy Ghost move. He was about teaching the Word of God by actually opening up the bible, reading and breaking down scripture. Sunday morning sermons resembled that of Wednesday night bible study and that was important to Symone. Like everyone who sought spiritual guidance, she wanted to know how the Kingdom of God system worked so she could put it to use and see results in her life. Bishop Reed helped his congregation find answers to why things weren't working in their lives instead of just offering excuses to explain away their lack or results.

"Symone Holmes!" Bishop Reed smiled brightly at Symone's presence. He stood up from behind his desk, walked around and met her at the door.

"How you doing, Bishop?" Symone hugged him and followed him into his office.

"Wonderful!" Bishop Reed extended his hand toward the empty seat in front of his desk. "I saw the draft. Congratulations."

Symone accepted his nonverbal invitation and sat down. "Thanks but you know better than I do that I wouldn't have made it without God's grace."

"Yes and your faith in His grace. They go hand in hand. If you didn't have faith in trusting that God's grace would get you here, you wouldn't be here."

Symone nodded. "I remember your sermons on interdependent relationship with God. I still listen to the CD every now and then."

"That's good. Listening to the Word is a form of meditation." Symone seemed lost in thought. Bishop Reed saw something was bothering her. "What brings you back this way?" he asked. "One would assume you'd be getting ready for the season."

"Yeah well, I may be sitting out this year."

"Are you hurt?" Bishop asked surprised.

"If it was only that simple," Symone said. "No, um, Imma stick around and help my mom get better."

Bishop was surprised but pleased. "What brought this about?"

"I just feel God's calling me to be here now. It's been four years, ya know since me and her last talked. Maybe we can try and work on changing that."

"Are you sure you're able to handle it now?"

"Yeah, I do. I admit, I've avoided the situation because it's easier to do that but I've grown over the past few years." Symone smiled and continued, "I have a wonderful woman in my life and regardless of what anybody says, God set our paths in motion for us to be together to get me ready for this moment. The love she has for me Bishop, it's something I never thought I'd feel from anyone. Her love has made me stronger, ya know. It's taught me how to love."

Bishop Reed smiled at the contentment in Symone's voice. "So where is she? When do I get to meet this blessing of yours?"

"Oh, she's still in North Carolina. I didn't want her in the middle of all this."

Bishop Reed interlocked his fingers and positioned his elbows on the desk. Symone read his mind as he fixed his gaze on her.

"It's not her fight, Bishop."

"And it's not yours alone, Symone. Remember what I told you when you came to me after your grandmother passed away?"

"That my pride would be my downfall but this ain't about pride, Bishop. Reggie's not used to the negative out lash. I don't want it to change her like it changed me."

"You just told me she's the reason you're ready to battle so why leave your greatest weapon locked away during the fight?"

"I just—if things go wrong here—"

"That's where trust in God comes in."

"I know but—"

"Do you know why we fail to see results, Symone?" Bishop Reed settled back in his cushioned chair.

"A lot of reasons," Symone replied.

"Yes, but there's one big reason most Christians struggle with."

Symone scratched the back of her head as she contemplated the question for a moment. "Disobedience?"

"Unbelief."

"Oh, I believe, Bishop. I got faith greater than most."

Bishop smiled, "Just because you have faith doesn't mean unbelief still can't exist."

"That—okay, say that again?" Symone sat up in the chair, leaned forward and listened intently.

"You agree we all have faith, correct?"

"Right."

"And it's our faith that goes out and gets the results."

"Right," Symone nodded, following Bishop Reed so far.

"Well, if you have fear, if you worry or if you carry the stress of something instead of giving it over to God, you also have unbelief. Unbelief and faith can coexist but unbelief keeps our faith hostage, not allowing it to go out and get the results God has promised us."

"I get it. It's kinda like an anchor."

Bishop Reed beamed, "That's right. Unbelief is an anchor drowning the power of your faith. If—" Bishop Reed snapped his fingers as he tried to recall Regina's name.

"Oh, Regina," Symone helped out.

"If Regina's one of the reasons you're able to face this situation with your mother, don't let unbelief limit the power she's infused in you."

"I'll think about it," Symone said.

"I'm always here when you need to talk."

Symone smirked at Bishop Reed's choice of words. Most people would've said '*if* you need to talk', not *when*. It was as though he knew she would be back.

"I'll more than likely be here the whole summer," Symone said.

"I look forward to seeing you in service then."

"After this little talk, I feel like I need to come Sunday, Wednesday and Friday night praise service, too."

"However the spirit moves you," Bishop Reed laughed.

Chapter 20

"Direct your children onto the right path, and when they are older, they will not leave it." ~ Proverbs 22:6

WE ALL HAVE THOSE Spidey senses that trigger an alarm in our bodies when something doesn't feel right. The hairs on the back of Symone's neck rose, waking her from her sleep. Her eyes immediately popped open and she found herself staring back at four small eyes, dancing with anticipation.

"Daddy! She's up!" Brianna yelled as she darted from the room.

"No I'm not," Symone grumbled.

Symone's two-year-old nephew stood at the head of the bed and watched her. He had a soft smile on his face as he breathed heavily through his mouth.

"Hey buddy," Symone said. "You need a baby wipe to take care of all that crust around your nose don't you? Your mouth gonna get dry you keep breathing like that."

Nathaniel remained silent but held up her watch, which he removed from the television stand when he first entered the room with his older sister.

"Can I see that?" Symone asked as she held out her hand.

Nathaniel exhaled heavily as though turning over the timepiece brought him emotional pain. Symone smiled at his theatrics then looked at the watch.

"You've got to be kidding me," Symone mumbled under her breath. It was six-forty in the morning. She closed her eyes and hoped she could fall back to sleep for a few more hours. She also hoped her resistance to get out of bed would bore Nathaniel and send him searching for another sleeping body to inspect.

Unfortunately, Nathaniel didn't get the hint. He stayed in the room, finding highlighters, pens and pencils to play with. His toddler gibberish prevented Symone from going back to sleep so she watched as he entertained himself with the writing instruments.

Sniff, sniff. Symone turned up her nose at the stench that began to consume the room.

"Nate Nate, you stink stink?"

Nathaniel exhaled loudly again. This time, frustration from being detected seeped through his tiny precious lips.

"Come here, Nate Nate."

Nathaniel put down his makeshift toys and stood to his feet. He walked over to Symone with his hands covering his eyes. Symone blinked repeatedly and took short breaths through her mouth to prevent the smell of poop from clogging up her nasal passages.

"Oh yeah, you need to be changed."

Symone sat up, took Nathaniel's small hand in hers and guided him to the living area where the rest of the family was.

"Your son needs to be changed," Symone said aloud.

"Have at it," Antoine said smiling.

"Uh no. I don't do diapers. Especially ones smelling that lethal."

Nicole called Nathaniel over to her and she checked his pamper. "Woo boy! What do you be eating?"

"It's all that milk he drinks," Antoine said. "Or the vegetables." Antoine turned to Symone and asked, "Have you ever known of a two-year-old to eat vegetables?"

"I was a vegetarian when I was pregnant with him," Nicole explained.

"And now all that good nutrition is exiting his body in the most potent fashion."

"Hush Antoine and come change him."

"I thought you were going to do it. You called him over there."

"I AM pregnant."

"What—" Antoine caught himself. He had been through this twice before. Arguing with your wife while she was pregnant with your child would always be a no-win situation. "C'mon over here, Nate Nate."

Nathaniel ran and jumped in his father's lap. He laughed as Antoine hung him upside down and carried him into the master bedroom.

"That's *your* brother," Nicole said smiling.

"Uh uh, he's all yours now."

Symone glanced in the living room and saw her seven-year-old niece watching *Dora the Explorer* while eating a bowl of *Lucky Charms*.

"Do they always get up this early?" Symone asked as she took a seat at the dining room table.

"Every morning."

"Why?"

"Because children don't know the meaning of sleeping in yet."

"It's time they learn."

Nicole laughed. "Nate Nate's usually the first up. When he's hungry, he gets out of bed, goes into the kitchen and takes out the milk. Then he comes into our room. If he sees we're not up, he goes and wakes up Bri."

Symone was impressed. "That boy's too smart for his own good."

"And just wait 'til this one gets here." Nicole pointed to her pregnant belly. "Three kids all under the age of ten. What were we thinking?"

"That it's best to get it out the way now," Antoine answered as he and Nathaniel reentered the room. "And the closer they are in age, the more they'll take care of each other as they get older."

"You really think so?" Symone asked skeptical.

"Bri already makes Nate Nate a bowl of cereal when they get up in the morning and gets his drinks and snacks." Antoine walked over to Nicole and rubbed her stomach. "When this little man gets here, I plan on having her helping with diapers."

"At seven, Ant?"

"Don't hate on my child labor. Back in the day, kids were plowing, cutting grass, milking cows—it's teaching them about responsibility and how to take care of each other at an early age."

"Um hmm."

"Hey, don't hate because I'm going old school to raise my kids. I'm preparing them for a harsh world, letting them know the only thing they can depend on is God and family."

"All right, Ant," Symone conceded. "I'm not arguing with you. It's too early and I haven't had breakfast yet."

"You hungry?" Nicole asked Symone.

"I can eat," Symone replied.

"You sound just like your brother. Why can't y'all just say yes?"

Antoine and Symone looked at each other and laughed. Nicole ignored them and headed to the kitchen to cook breakfast.

"So, what are you getting into today?" Antoine asked.

"First, I'm taking my butt back to sleep for a couple more hours—"

"You better lock that door then because Nate Nate will be right back up in there."

"I noticed him playing with pens earlier. He left-handed?"

Antoine nodded. "Yep, just like you and he loves basketball. Watch this."

Antoine called to Nathaniel and had him bring a foam basketball with him. Antoine interlocked his fingers and turned his arms into a wide hoop. Nathaniel's face immediately lit up and he dunked the ball on Antoine's arms.

"Tut-down!" Nathaniel shouted at the successful goal.

"Touchdown?" Symone repeated with a smile.

"Hey, I said he liked basketball. I didn't say he understood the verbiage associated with the game."

"But touchdown?"

"He's two. I'll get him right by the time he's able to play," Antoine winked.

Chapter 21

"As iron sharpens iron, so a friend sharpens a friend." ~ Proverbs 27:17

"DIDN'T TAKE YOU LONG to make contact this time. I guess you learned your lesson."

"Well, I know you already knew I was in town so figured might as well. Couldn't risk you coming by the house busting down doors like you SWAT or something."

Symone stood before former teammates and old friends Kyra and Chief. Kyra jerked her head to the side to remove the strands of hair tickling her forehead. The rest of her long brown hair was pulled back in a ponytail.

It didn't matter what was going on in their lives, after five o'clock, both Kyra and Chief could always be found at the outdoor courts at Fairlawn Recreation Center. Making contact was the easy part. Thanks to their history, having a rational conversation was a very different matter.

"So, you two gonna kiss and make up already?" Chief asked. She repositioned the white headband higher on her brow to catch the beads of sweat that started to form. "I'm ready to play ball."

Kyra sat on the fourth row of the silver metal bleachers, placing her almost eye level with Symone. She stared at Symone waiting for a sign that they did not have to do this dance but Symone did not budge.

"She's my sister, Sy," Kyra finally said.

"I know. Didn't make it hurt any less though."

"So, what you wanna do? Take me on Ricki, Jerry, Oprah? You need to learn how to let some shit go."

Symone frowned. "You're so freaking garbage, Kyra. I mean, you were my best friend. I couldn't even get a head's up?"

"Hell naw!"

Symone was caught off guard by Kyra's out lash. "Why not?"

"'Cause I was pissed at you that's why." Kyra climbed down off the bleachers and got right in Symone's face. "You broke Kid's heart, man."

"I—"

Kyra sighed and relaxed her defensive stance. "Don't get me wrong, I love Regina. I think she's the best thing to happen to your punk ass but it all came at a hefty price."

"I get that now," Symone said, lowering her head.

"Do you? 'Cause it seem to me you still holding a grudge over shit *you* caused. It's been five years, Sy." Kyra tapped Symone on her chest and commanded, "Let it go."

Kyra moved passed her to the empty court in front of them. Symone rubbed the back of her neck and closed her eyes tight. She knew Kyra was right. She created the situation and she couldn't be mad because nobody reacted the way she wanted them to.

"So we good?" Chief asked, not sure if the problem had been resolved yet.

"I've always been good," Kyra said.

Symone turned to them and replied, "Yeah, we straight."

"Cool." Chief tossed the basketball to Symone.

"You need to talk with Kid, too," Kyra said to Symone. "Cut her some slack."

"Already did."

Kyra and Chief looked at each other with impressed expressions on their faces.

"Maybe she *is* growing up," Chief said smiling.

"You think?"

Symone tossed the ball back to Chief but with a little more zip. "Whatever."

"Ooo, she still got some fire."

Kyra smiled and taunted, "Those hands ain't too precious to play pick up ball are they?"

"They're worth more than your whole year's salary," Symone taunted back. "And pick up ball these days are like practice."

"Why don't you save that trash talking for the jokers we're 'bout to squash?"

"You know me. I got enough to serve everybody."

AFTER PLAYING AND WINNING three half-court three on three games against male competitors, Symone, Kyra and Chief decided to take a break.

"I haven't had that much fun in years!" Chief laughed. "I love busting dudes balls on the courts."

"That's what they get for thinking we don't belong," Kyra said. She turned to their victims still licking their wounds and shouted, "Y'all might've built these courts with all those bricks y'all were throwing up but" with her arms outstretched, "this is our home!"

"Who's the trash talker now?" Symone said to Chief with a gentle nudge.

"She's definitely been picking up the slack since you left."

Kyra waved off the bantering from the men and sat on the bleachers next to Symone. Chief handed them both bottled water she retrieved from her gym bag.

Chief gulped down half her bottle. "Ahhh, that's refreshing."

"What are you, auditioning for a freaking commercial?"

"Shut up, Symone 'fore I take back that water and make you drink that brown slush coming out that fountain over there."

"Like the time you made me drink bourbon?"

Kyra laughed aloud at the old memory. "That was funny as shit! You just kept yelling, 'my chest is burning, my chest is burning'."

"And y'all wonder why I'm not a drinker now."

"Oh, Kyra, remember the time we tricked her into watching that porno!"

Symone shook her head as the two laughed at her innocence.

"She covered her eyes when the guy pulled his pee pee out!" Chief laughed so hard she started to cry.

"His wiener was so small it looked like a little Vienna sausage," Symone said.

That statement caused Chief to laugh even harder. "Stop it! I can't breathe!"

"That's all right. I got you both back eventually."

Kyra gained composure first and responded, "Yeah you did. I think I did more chores at your house than I did at my own."

"I'm surprised you didn't call us over this time to help so you could escape your mom's wrath," Chief added. "Sorry. I didn't mean—"

"I know, it's cool."

The comment flashed forward the group back to the present.

"Well, I better get going," Kyra said standing up. "Some of us don't have the luxury of having the summer off like you too."

"Don't blame it on work. You know Sam will have you ass in a sling if you were late for dinner," Chief teased.

"At least I got me somebody cooking me dinner," Kyra shot back.

"I got me somebody all right," Chief began. "And your mom's Yuca always be on point."

Kyra waved off Chief's last joke and tossed her shoulder bag over the headrest onto the backseat of her car.

"I better get going too," Chief said stretching. "Don't forget to call me about working with my team," she reminded Symone.

"I won't but I'll probably only have time to do a day, not a whole week."

"That's fine. I know the girls will love to work with you."

Symone laughed. "They probably don't even know how I am."

"Trust me," Chief patted Symone on the back, "you're a female basketball player from Norfolk who went pro. These girls definitely know who you are."

Chapter 22

"Even if my father and mother abandon me,
the LORD will hold me close." ~ Psalms 27:10

SYMONE PARKED IN FRONT of her parents' home
not sure of what to expect. She called her father when she
first woke up and told him to prepare her mom for
training that morning. Symone sat with Antoine the past
few nights designing a lightweight workout plan to help
their mother regain function to the right side of her body
using household items, stretching and kinesthetic
movements. Symone would work with her three times a
week, showing her father each technique so he could
work with her mom at least one other day out of the
week.

Symone walked into the house and found her
father sitting on the beige leather sofa alone. His eyes
were puffy and the lines that etched his forehead and
mouth were more pronounced than usual. The green and
white family reunion shirt he wore was well past worn
and the brown khaki pants he cut into shorts himself
were frayed at the edges.

"Where's mom?" Symone asked.

"In the bedroom," he said wearily. "She refuses to
come out."

Symone placed her hands on her hips. "Of
course. I wouldn't have expected anything less." Symone

clicked her tongue on the bridge of her mouth as she thought of her next course of action. "If she wants to act like the child, I guess I'll have to be the parent." Symone exhaled slowly as she made her way down the hall to the master bedroom where her mother held herself hostage.

Symone opened the bedroom door and found her mother in bed watching television.

"We're supposed to be training today, ma."

Paula did not respond.

"Don't you want to get better?"

Still, no response.

"I can be stubborn, too, ya know. I took the whole season off from playing ball so I'll be here all summer, longer if you force my hand."

Paula continued to ignore Symone's presence by channel surfing.

"You're gonna have to talk to me sooner or later." Symone took two steps into the room but her mom rolled over, turning her back on her. "Fine but I'll be back." She paused at the door and added, "I'm not giving up on you."

Symone closed the door and leaned against it. She wiped away a tear and gathered herself. It was going to be hard to break down years of resentment but she was up for the challenge.

Symone started toward the living room when she saw that the bedroom door across from her mother's room was cracked. She peeked inside and found the room filled with bookshelves and oversized plastic bins.

"I guess this became the storage room," she said to herself.

Symone slowly turned counterclockwise inventorying every visible item in the room. Her eyes fell upon an oversized purple photo album extending beyond the normal 8x11 books on the bookshelf. Symone pulled the photo album down from the bookshelf and removed the basket full of clean towels and white underclothes out the wicker chair so she could sit down.

Symone thumbed through the album, smiling at baby pictures and laughing at grade school portraits. The trip down memory lane also had her revisit times that weren't as pleasant, pictures not stored in a photo album but locked away in the deep valleys of her mind.

****

"THIS IS NOT YOU!" Paula screamed.

"How do you know?" Symone cried back.

"Because I didn't raise you to be like this!"

Symone didn't understand why every time she and her mother argued about her sexuality, child rearing was her mother's number one defense.

"Why do you keep saying that? How you've raised me got nothing to do with me being gay!"

"It has everything to do with it! I did better by you than this."

"So I owe you now?" Symone said with more attitude than she anticipated.

Paula was taken back by the question and Symone's tone of voice but responded, "Yes, you do. I deserve to have a daughter who acts like a lady. One who likes to put on makeup and wear a dress, for goodness sakes!"

"Those things don't make me a lady," Symone replied.

"Walking around looking like a little boy sure doesn't either."

"But ma—"

Paula held up her hand to silence Symone. "I just don't understand why you'd want to do this to yourself, Symone. Why you'd want to hurt the family, hurt me like this."

"You think this is easy for me? You think I wanna live like this? You don't know what I'm feeling and how much it hurts me to see you hurting" Symone poked herself repeatedly in the chest, "because of me. You don't know how this is killing me. I don't

wanna hurt you. You're my mother and I love you but I can't stop your pain or mine because I can't change who I am."

Paula shook her head emphatically. "No, no I don't believe it."

"Ma, I'm sorry but I can't help that when I look at a guy I don't feel nothing but when I look at a girl—"

"Don't you dare say it."

"When I look at a girl, I feel she's the most beautiful thing God created."

SLAP! The coldness from Paula's hand stung the side of Symone's face.

"Don't you ever use God's name with your sickness."

Through soft cries, Symone replied, "By His stripes—I am healed."

****

SYMONE PLACED HER HAND against the side of her face to warm her cheek from the thought of the icy slap. That was the one and only time her mother every hit her. She removed a few of her favorite pictures from the photo album and placed them in the pocket of her gym shorts. Symone did not have many pictures from her childhood so she decided she would use those pictures to start her own photo album. Give her something to show her own kids one day.

As she placed the photo album back on the bookshelf, she found an, *As I Grow Up* scrapbook. She never saw the book before so spent a little time flipping through it.

The first page was titled, Birth, and it had Symone's birth picture taped to it. The page had a pocket where Symone found a copy of her birth certificate, a picture of her inked baby footprints and a pink hospital bracelet with the name 'Baby Simpson' etched on it.

Symone sat back down and analyzed each page thereafter. The book had a page for every important moment of a child's life, from baby's first steps to first loss tooth to first day of school to sweet sixteen, first car and prom. The latter part of the book consisted of high school graduation and first day of college. There were even pages for wedding and grandchildren.

"Symone?" Symone looked up and saw her dad standing in the doorway. "You went to check on your mom—"

"Yeah, she's not having it today. I'll figure something out though." Symone lifted the book and asked, "Where did this come from?"

"Your mother bought that when she found out she was pregnant with you. It helps parents keep track of all the highlights of their child's life."

"How come I've never seen it before now?"

"She always kept up with it. Stuffing your report cards and perfect attendance certificates in the little pockets. She must've put it away when—when you left."

Symone skipped forward to twelfth grade and saw that it resembled that of eleventh grade. There were no pictures or mementos stuffed in the sleeve. Symone was hurt when her mother didn't show up for her graduation. It was that day Symone realized she was truly on her own and she had to trust in what she knew up to that point to get her where she wanted to be in the future.

"Can I keep this?" Symone asked.

"Yeah, sure."

Symone was still lost in the pages of the book so Frederick left the room, allowing her to be alone with her thoughts.

Chapter 23

"He canceled the record of the charges
against us and took it away by nailing it to the
cross." ~ Colossians 2:14

"AND HOW'S EVERYTHING GOING today?"

Bishop settled in his chair as Symone sat in the chair opposite his desk. She called him thirty minutes prior and asked if she could meet earlier than her two o'clock appointed time.

Symone slouched in the auburn colored armchair and said, "My mom refused to come out of her room the other day. She wouldn't even look at me."

"I'm sorry, Symone."

"I just don't get what her problem is. At first I felt guilty but now I think I'm just pissed." Symone looked across the mahogany desk at Bishop with guilty eyes and said, "Sorry."

Bishop Reed just smiled. "What are you upset about?"

Symone leaned forward, cleared her throat and began, "I found this book, it's kinda like a scrap book where parents can document important events in their child's life. I never saw the book before, didn't even know it existed but it was like—I dunno. Almost like my life had been mapped out before I had a chance to live it and she made the necessary changes along the way."

"And what about this makes you mad?"

"It's my life, Bishop. She can't be mad at me because I didn't follow her plan." Symone slumped back down in the chair. "Parents don't understand how hard it is for a child to come to them and tell them, 'mom, dad, I'm not who you envisioned me to be'."

"We feel that way as Christians too. Sometimes we feel we have to come before God already perfect and because we're not, we refuse to give ourselves to Him completely or we feel He doesn't love us. We anticipate bad things happening to us, thinking it's God punishing us for our wrongdoings but we forget or maybe we don't even know that God took His wrath out on Jesus at the cross. That was the purpose for Jesus birth. So all the bad stuff we did, do and will do, he paid the price for all of it already. Our sins are forgiven. Jesus was the final sacrifice so we can go to the Father and not have to hide in shame. We can go to the Father and not have to be perfect. Jesus' blood took care of it all."

"Parents should be the same way but they're not."

"No, unfortunately they're not."

"I read online that one in four gay youth will become homeless the day they come out to their parents. One in four, Bishop."

"That's an extremely disturbing statistic."

"I know right. At first, I was like, 'naw, that can't be right' but I almost lived it. I'm finding out now that if it wasn't for my dad, I would've been one of those homeless teens. How selfish, hard, cold do you have to be as a parent to put your own cares before your child and worse, use God's name to justify it? God didn't put anything before us. Not even his own son Jesus."

"Human beings are different."

"Well, we need to do better."

"We do."

"Parents need to realize their child is not trying to hurt them or piss them off. They need to realize it's not about them at all. I want to tell them all to get over themselves."

Bishop saw the wheels turning in Symone's head. "What are you thinking?" he asked.

"It's nothing." Bishop had that look on his face so Symone shared, "A couple of weeks ago, I was out with Regina and some of her friends and one of them asked me what causes was I gonna fight for now that I'm a celebrity."

"Causes?"

"Yeah, gay rights stuff. I never really thought about that stuff."

"And why is that?"

"I just never did but I think this is something I want to look into tackling, maybe."

"Educating parents—"

"Or just talking to them period, letting them know that their kids are getting bullied for who they are and who they love at school, at work, everywhere they go. They don't need to be bullied at home, too. Home is the one place love should always be present no matter what."

"That sounds like a great cause to tackle," Bishop Reed said.

"I wonder if there's anything like that out already. I mean, I know they have PFLAG."

"PFLAG?"

"Parents for Lesbians and Gays but those are the parents that have accepted their kids. I need a program that's trying to reach the parents who haven't."

"Or maybe you could start one."

Symone nodded in agreement. She felt this was definitely an area of interest she could pursue while she was on hiatus from the league.

"Thanks a lot Bishop."

Bishop Reed waved goodbye as Symone headed out the church to her car. She was so excited to have a cause she called Regina to see what she thought of the idea.

"Hello?"

"Hey baby. You busy?"

"Not really. Things are pretty slow here in the office."

Symone thought about telling Regina about the tough time she was having with her mom but decided against it. She wanted to focus on the good news. "Guess what? I just finished talking with my old Bishop and he sparked an idea in me."

"An idea?"

"Yeah, for a cause I can stand for in the gay community."

"That's why you called me?"

Symone pulled the phone away from her ear and looked at it confused. "Why you sound pissed?"

"I don't know. Maybe because I've been calling you for the past few days and you haven't called me back."

"But I texted you to let you know why I couldn't talk."

"Text?" Regina took a deep breath to keep calm. "If I call you, you should respect me enough to call me back."

"Respect? What—" Symone huffed. "You know what, fine. The next time I'm in the middle of talking to Ant or training my mom and you call, I'll be sure to—"

"Don't okay." Regina cut her off sharply. "Speaking of Antoine, did you talk to him about me staying there?"

"I haven't got my mom working with me yet, Reggie."

"I didn't ask you that."

"If my mom refuses to let me help her, I won't be here long enough for you to take a leave of absence from your job. Come on now. You said you had my back on this. I can't fight her and fight you, too. Give me a break, okay?"

Regina let out a deep sigh. "You're right. I'm sorry."

"I don't like us fighting, Reggie and we've been doing a lot of it lately."

"I know. I hate it too." Regina paused and Symone could hear voices in the background. "I have to go, baby."

"Okay, I'll call you later tonight. I promise."

"Okay," Regina smiled softly. "I love you."

"I love you, too."

Symone hung up and exhaled loudly. She narrowly escaped with her excuse to Regina about her joining her in Virginia. Symone considered everything Bishop Reed told her during their first meeting but something still kept her from including Regina in this particular part of her life.

Chapter 24

"So let us come boldly to the throne of our gracious God. There we will receive his mercy, and we will find grace to help us when we need it most." ~ Hebrews 4:16

"SO TELL ME SYMONE," Nicole began, "how was Antoine when he was a kid?"

"Y'all've been married for how long and he hasn't told you yet?" Symone bounced Nathaniel on her knee and said jokingly, "Aw, you've been duped."

"I can hear you."

Antoine sat on the floor in front of the black suede sectional sofa. Brianna sat behind him with a brush and hair berets. She grabbed a couple of his locs with her tiny hands and started plaiting them.

"I'm joking. Nah, Ant was an awesome big brother," Symone said. "I remember one time when I was being picked on by the neighborhood bully—"

"Jason!" Antoine shouted.

"Yep." Antoine laughed as Symone told the story, "Ant thought it was time Jason finally got a taste of his own medicine."

"I remember what happened."

"Can I finish?"

Antoine held up his hands in surrender.

"Antoine and I walked down the street to Jason's house where he was terrorizing his little brothers in the front yard. We started taunting him, doing the 'na na na boo boo' and the whole nine." Nicole laughed as Symone continued, more animated, "Jason took off running after us. We were hopping fences and clearing ditches. We led him across the field toward the back of our house. We knew he was seeing red 'cause he was yelling and screaming, saying he was gonna kill us when he caught us." Symone leaned forward as the plot thickened. "We cut across our backyard, carefully lowering our heads to avoid the green-wired clothesline that was camouflaged by the branches and leaves from the huge oak trees the clothesline was attached to. Jason followed our trail to a 'T' and—"

"No," Nicole anticipated the worse.

"Yes!" Antoine shouted.

Symone ignored them both and continued with the story, "Next thing we know, the clothesline caught him right up under his neck, lifted him clean off his feet and slammed him down flat on the ground."

"Ooo!" Nicole flinched. "I know that had to hurt."

"He laid there so still I thought we killed him," Antoine added. "Then I walked over and saw him gasping for air. Joker literally had the wind knocked out of him."

"All of a sudden, Ant grows a huge set. He walks over to Jason who's still laid out," Symone got up and towered over top Antoine. She put her hands on her hips and said, "Ant was like, 'keep messing with my sister and we'll booby trap this whole neighborhood. You'll think you're in a spoof version of *Home Alone* by the time we get through with you'."

"And he didn't bother you no more, did he?" Antoine said. Symone held out her hand and Antoine slapped her five. "All right then," he stated proudly.

"Aww, my Ant was a brave big brother," Nicole cooed.

"Don't get it twisted though. I was praying that stunt would work."

"You were scared?"

"Baby, that white boy was big." Nicole and Symone laughed as Antoine carried on, "Like some cornbread fed, tracker pulling, redneck deer hunting type of big."

"But you put him in his place, didn't you?"

"SHO NUFF!"

"Ah!" Symone yelled. "That's my movie." Symone made a couple of karate moves with her hands and said, "Bruce Leroy. The Master."

"I got *The Last Dragon* on DVD, sis."

"Shut up! You gotta let me borrow it!"

Nicole watched in admiration as Symone and Antoine reminisced on old times. She loved their interaction and wondered why she hadn't seen more of it in the past.

"I can tell you two were close growing up," Nicole said.

"Very," Antoine corrected.

"So why am I just now seeing the two of you hanging out like this?"

Symone thought she was better suited to explain so she answered, "After my parents found out I was gay, things changed. Ant had already graduated from high school so he wasn't around to see a lot of it."

"Me not being there didn't mean you had to deal with it alone, Sy," Antoine said seriously. "I told you I got your back."

"You were away at college Ant, battling a knee injury and trying to get back in the starting lineup on the team. And a lot more happened then you know—"

"Like what?"

"It doesn't matter now—"

"Yes it does."

"Daddy you keep moving," Brianna whined.

"We both were in some type of survival mode and surviving got in the way of us staying connected," Symone stated.

Antoine was not satisfied and refused to let it go. "All right kids, bed time."

Brianna and Nathaniel whined because they wanted to stay up longer but it was already past ten 'o clock.

Nicole saw that Antoine wanted alone time with Symone so she helped the kids into the next room to prepare them for bed.

"So what is it that I don't know," Antoine asked.

"I don't wanna get into it now, Antoine. It's—it's old news now."

"Obviously not."

Symone let out an exaggerated sigh. Her back was stiff so she grabbed one of the decorative pillows from the sofa. She lay on the floor face up and placed the pillow under her knees to elevate her legs, relieving the pressure from her midsection.

Once she was comfortable, she warned, "Okay but I warned you."

"Just talk," Antoine demanded.

"Fine. Short version, mom went to dad's family on how to," she used air quotations, "'handle' me being gay and they told her to kick me out."

Antoine jumped to his feet. "What? Who?"

"Everybody."

"And you know this for sure?"

"I figured his side of the family disowned me but I didn't know they tried to get mom and dad to do it too. But yeah, I got confirmation from a reliable source within the family." Symone thought about telling Antoine that her source was Uncle Ward. She knew Uncle Ward wouldn't mind but she felt it was best for him to remain anonymous for moment.

"Why didn't you tell me?" Antoine asked as he rested on the sofa behind her.

"What could you do? You were in college. Besides, it's not like I couldn't take care of myself." In an effort to lighten the mood, Symone replied jokingly, "Thank god ma put me in that calligraphy class. I guess at the end of the day she really was preparing me to make it on my own."

Antoine ignored Symone's pathetic attempt at humor. "I just can't believe it. You still should've told me."

"Honestly Ant, I was scared to tell you."

"Why?"

Symone rolled over and sat with her legs stretched out in front of her. She hesitated then said, "This was around the time you met Nicole. You were changing your life, focusing on being a better God-fearing man. I didn't want you to get mad at them and stunt your spiritual growth."

Antoine looked at her unimpressed. "Now you know that would've never happened."

"You never know. We were different people back then, ya know."

"True, but still—I don't know." Antoine leaned back into the sofa and ran his hands through his locs as he tried to absorb the information.

"I was also scared that—because you were getting into the Word more, I thought—I dunno—I was afraid you would agree with them."

Antoine sat up and squared his body to Symone. "I would've never agreed for them to kick you out, Sy. That's crazy."

"I didn't know!" Symone exhaled loudly and stood to her feet. "All I knew was that I didn't wanna risk losing you, too. I—I just couldn't handle that."

Antoine saw how much this conversation was hurting Symone. He walked over and gave her a big hug. "You can't lose me, you hear?" Symone wiped her tears and nodded. Antoine looked at her and asked, "Is that why you never went to any of the family functions?"

"Ant, half those things I didn't even know about. Nobody invited me."

"Dang." Antoine was disappointed and angry but he tried his best not to show it. He wandered over to the sofa and sat on the armrest.

"It's like I said before," Symone took a seat in the wooden kitchen chair, "it's all old news. I've forgiven and forgotten."

"Really?"

"They made it easy by cutting me off completely. Most of the family I haven't spoken to in close to six years, more of them I haven't seen in longer than that. It's easy to forget those who make themselves nonexistent in your life."

"But what about mom and dad?" Antoine asked.

Symone shrugged. "Ya know, they're my parents. I can't forget them."

"So what you going to do?"

"Just keep following the Word in honoring them and let the Lord handle the rest. I mean, that's why I'm here instead of playing basketball, ya know. I can only control my actions, not theirs."

Chapter 25

"So be strong and courageous, all you who put
your hope in the LORD!" ~ Psalms 31:24

"I DID WHAT YOU asked," Frederick said to Symone
when she entered the house. "She hasn't eaten all
morning."

"Good."

Symone knew if she was going to get her mom to
work with her, she would need her dad's help. She called
and asked him not to feed Paula her breakfast in the
bedroom. Symone needed her mom out of bed and out
of the bedroom. Hunger would help her achieve that
goal.

Symone looked at her watch and saw it was eight-
thirty. According to her dad, her mom usually ate
breakfast at eight. Symone figured they had an hour,
maybe ninety minutes before she came searching for
food.

"So we just wait?" Frederick asked.

Symone looked at her dad and nodded. They sat
on the beige leather sofa in silence watching *SportsCenter*.
Frederick turned the volume up on the television when
they aired highlights to the WNBA preseason games.

*"The Sting suffered another tough loss to the Houston
Comets, this time in overtime. They have now lost all of*

their preseason games leading into their season opener at home against the Washington Mystics. Charlotte hoped this season would be one of rebuilding to climb back in the hunt as contenders in the East but they haven't had enough firepower to get over the hump in these close games. All of their preseason loses have come by way of five points or fewer. The lost of their rookie sensation, Symone Holmes, has left the team shorthanded in the scoring department. Symone Holmes, Charlotte's number one draft pick, elected to forego her rookie season to attend to a personal family matter."

Symone rolled her eyes at the report. She tried her best to avoid watching any sports programs for this very reason. She knew she put the team in a tough position and she missed playing ball dearly. Watching the games would only be putting herself through torture.

"Let's go over the training plan me and Antoine came up with," Symone suggested hoping to get her mind off basketball. She unzipped the navy blue fatigued book bag she brought with her and emptied the contents on the floor. She handed her dad the workout plan and explained each items purpose in the training.

"So, soup cans, soda cans—"

"Water bottles, dad. No sodas."

"What's the difference if she's using them as weights?"

"As she gets stronger, we're going to move her to real weights and I don't want y'all having a bunch of soda in the house. Both of you need to drink more water anyway. Help with your cholesterol."

Frederick nodded. "All this seems easy enough."

"Now if we can just get her out here so I can show you what she needs to do with them."

Frederick used the INFO button on the remote control to check the time on the television. "It's only been twenty minutes so we still may have awhile."

Symone extended her legs, leaned forward and stretched her back. "Well I have until two so I got time."

The awkward silence looming between Symone and her father bothered her. There was obvious tension in the room but it only existed on Symone's shoulders. Thanks to Uncle Ward, she knew her father came to her defense when the family found out she was gay. What she did not understand was why he never said anything about it to her.

"Uncle Ward came to see me when I was in Charlotte."

Frederick chuckled under his breath. "He still got that truck on the road? I thought he would've retired by now."

"He says he loves it. Gives him time to have his own man time." Frederick chuckled again as Symone thought of a way to ease the conversation to a more pressing topic. "He told me about Lil Cas and Aunt Maddy."

"Oh," Frederick said in surprised.

"How come you never told me you stood up for me when your family was trying to convince you and mom to put me out?"

The question caught Frederick by surprise. Symone wasn't sure if he was more surprised by the fact that she knew about the family conspiracy or that she knew he defied them.

"It wasn't my place to ask you about your business," he finally said. "I wanted you to come to us when you were comfortable talking to us about it."

"How could I be comfortable if I didn't know, especially the way mom's been—"

"Your mom was heartbroken, still is, I suppose."

"Yeah but—I dunno. It's like, nobody cared enough to ask me how I felt. Everyone assumed I chose this or I wanted this." Symone paused to fight back tears.

"One day I was a part of this big family and the next, I had nobody. That's tough to swallow at fifteen, dad."

Frederick lowered his eyes in shame. "I'm sorry about that. I guess I felt guilty in a way, blaming myself for you turning out like this."

"Teaching me about cars and playing sports didn't make me gay."

"I know it didn't but—none of this was easy for anybody."

"Yeah but moms are supposed to still love their daughters regardless—"

"Your mother does love you, Symone." Frederick cleared his throat and continued, "When your mom and I got married, all she talked about was having a little girl. She grew up with four brothers so she didn't have that girl bond. I believe she wanted to share that with you and you being—liking girls ruined that dream for her."

"Just 'cause I'd rather play with a wolverine action figure than a Barbie doll—" Symone shook her head.

"Your mom—she felt robbed," Frederick admitted. "Prom, wedding, grandkids—"

"She still could've—she still can have all that, dad. That's what I'm trying to get her to understand."

"I just wanted you to know what she's been going through, Symone. I don't want you to keep thinking she's a bad mom."

Symone sighed guiltily, "I don't think that. I just—I know she's afraid. All of her actions have been based in fear." Symone settled wearily into the sofa and rambled on, "Maybe she's afraid we've lost too much time or that I'm mad at her. She always throws grandma in my face so maybe she thinks she failed her somehow. I dunno."

"Or maybe she thinks she failed you." Symone looked at her father in surprise as he continued, "You already know this life isn't an easy life to live, Symone. Seeing you in the hospital a few years ago scared us both half to death. Your life is harder than it should be now and she may feel that's her fault."

"Then why she wanna put me out?" Symone asked. "Wouldn't've made sense to want to hold on to me, protect me?"

Frederick hesitated but answered, "Some people can't face their failures. They either dump it and start over or dump it and try to forget it ever happened."

"I'm not a failure," Symone said defensively.

"No, you're not and your mother knows that." Frederick nodded to himself and confessed, "She pushed you away because she thought you'd do better without her."

"What?"

"She knew it was going to take her some time to get past it. She didn't want you to have to suffer while she went through her healing process."

Symone closed her eyes and wiped at the tears that escaped. "But I needed her. I needed you both."

Frederick struggled to respond. Fortunately for him, Paula's electric scooter was on the move. She parked at the threshold of the hallway and living room. "I'm hungry," she stated plainly.

Frederick looked at Symone. She nodded and he got up and headed to the kitchen. Symone thought over the conversation she just had with her dad as she looked at her mom. She never thought to put herself in her mom's shoes. Just like her mom, she only saw the situation from one side, her own. To change that, Symone knew they needed time together to talk but her mother was making that hard. She needed an incentive to lower Paula's defenses.

"I know you don't want me here, ma," Symone began, "and to be honest, part of me would rather be living my life playing basketball."

"Then go."

"I will, as soon as you're better." Paula gave Symone a hard glare. "I'll make you a deal." Symone cocked her head to crack her neck. "You let me train you, help you get better and once you're able to take care of yourself again, I'll leave and never come back."

Frederick overheard the bargain. "Wait a minute," he said. "I'm not—"

"It's not your choice, dad." Symone turned back to her mother. "I want you to get better and I know I can help you. If after that time, you still don't want to see me anymore, I'll get out of your life forever."

"Symone—"

"Dad, please." Symone didn't want to negotiate. She knew this was the only way to overcome Paula's barrier of stubbornness. "So, what do you say, ma? We training today?"

Chapter 26

"Love does no wrong to others, so love fulfills the requirements of God's law." ~ Romans 13:10

SYMONE STOOD OUTSIDE KIDERA'S apartment door trying to shake the nerves out of her hands. Their first meeting was on neutral ground but today was different. Today, Symone was on Kidera's territory.

Symone still stood at the door trying to gather herself when the door suddenly opened.

"You know my apartment faces the street and I can see you," Kidera said smiling at Symone.

Symone stuffed her hands deep into her jean pockets. "Oh."

"¿Vas a entrar?"

"You inviting me in?"

Kidera rolled her eyes and pushed the door open wide. Symone followed her in and closed the door behind her. She watched Kidera and admired how good the years had been to her. Kidera was still short and thin but her bust line and backside were fuller. Her brown wavy hair finally met her waist, a goal Kidera wanted to accomplish ever since Symone had known her.

"I don't think Regina would appreciate you checking out mí culo," Kidera teased as she twitched her hips.

Symone smiled in embarrassment then surveyed the apartment. "So, you stay here alone?" she asked while inspecting photos on the windowsill.

"If you're asking if I'm dating someone, the answer's no."

Symone hunched her shoulders as if she wasn't interested. "What's up with all the books?"

"I'm in grad school studying Psychology." Symone looked impressed as Kidera continued, "I thought I should learn more about human behavior before getting into another serious relationship."

Symone cut her eyes toward Kidera. She knew the last statement was a jab at her and their previous relationship.

"Look, I didn't come here to start an argument with you, okay? I just—you know what, nevermind."

Symone moved to the door when Kidera words stopped her.

"I'm sorry, okay. I guess I didn't get everything out the first time."

"You and Kyra keep telling me I need to let it go and I'm trying. I really am but if y'all keep taking shots at me—"

"I get it," Kidera said, not letting her finish. "Starting today, clean slate."

Symone watched Kidera as she walked over with her hand extended. Symone thought for a moment then shook hands.

Kidera smiled. "Are you going to tell me what's wrong now?" she asked heading back into the kitchen.

"How you—nevermind." Symone plopped down on the deep purple micro suede loveseat and let out an extended sigh. "It's my brother and his family."

"Ant?"

"Don't get me wrong, they're great but oh my god! The noise is driving me crazy and why do they wake up so early!"

"Who? Your brother?"

"No, the kids?"

Kidera smiled with the spoon of honey-roasted peanut butter in her mouth. "They're kids, Symone."

"I've never known children to produce that much noise and it's only two of them."

"That's because you're not around children and when you are, they're in public. Kids do more damage when they're in their own comfort zone."

"They stare at me while I'm sleeping, Kid."

"What are you talking about?"

"I wake up every morning with Brianna and Nate Nate looking right dead at me. If I was a trained killer, those kids would be goners by now."

"Lock the bedroom door."

"I did!"

Kidera laughed. She walked into the living room with two saucers, each holding a peanut butter and jelly sandwich. She handed one of the plates to Symone and sat the other on the coffee table before returning to the kitchen.

"So, your niece and nephew are ninja stealth—"

"That I can look past though but the noise…I'm used to my own space with peace and quiet."

"What are you talking about your own space? You live with Regina. You lived with me."

"Yeah, but y'all not unnecessarily loud for no reason."

"And I say again, they're kids." Kidera placed a glass of water on a coaster in front of Symone and a glass of milk on the coaster in front of her. She sat down in the matching purple chair and took a bite of her sandwich.

"Bri's all of seven and that girl can talk." Symone paused to take a bite of her sandwich, "and you know if I'm saying she can talk, she can talk."

"Sounds like she has the Holmes' blood."

"Not funny. Now Nate Nate, with his cute spoiled self…that boy cries every time Ant leaves the room and he is stubborn as all get out."

"Did you tell Ant any of this?"

"I told them both."

"And what did they say?"

"We know."

Kidera laughed harder.

"I don't understand what's so funny."

Kidera sipped her milk and said, "You."

Symone sat the empty plate on the end table next to her, laid her head on the back of the cushion and closed her eyes. "I just want one good night's sleep."

"Why don't you stay here?"

Symone's head popped up. "Huh?"

"I have an extra bedroom. During the day, I'm in class so just stay here."

"Nah, I'm good," Symone said without hesitation.

"O-kay—"

"I'm just saying, Regina's already mad at me for coming up here without her. Staying here would add *a lot* more fuel to the fire."

"So you're just going to stay in a hotel for the next few months?"

"If I have to."

"Es estúpido, Symone."

"It ain't like I don't have the money."

"That's not the point. You have other places you can stay."

"Where? Not with my parents. Definitely not with your sister."

"Why don't you just talk to Regina and—"

Symone stood to her feet. "Oh yeah, okay." Symone pretended to talk on the phone. "Hey baby, I know you're still mad at me for lying to you and I'm sorry about that. By the way, you mind if I bunk with my ex-girlfriend?" Symone gave Kidera the 'yeah right' look.

"Okay fine. What if you just—I don't know. Just stay here on occasion."

"I don't even know what that means."

"It means when you're stressed and you need a break, just come here."

"But I'd still be spending the night."

"Then come over during the day when I'm in class. Get a few hours nap then go work with your mom or play ball or whatever it is you do while you're on break."

Symone sat on the back of the loveseat and thought about it while Kidera cleaned up the living room.

"I know this thing with your mom is hard for you, Symone. You know if anybody knows, I know. I'm not trying to make a move on you or anything like that. I know you better than that. I'm just trying to be a friend."

"I guess that wouldn't be so bad," Symone finally said. "Especially if you're in class and it's not an overnight thing. Reggie should be good with that."

"Good. Then it's settled."

"Wait, how am I gonna get in if you're not here?"

"I'll get you a key."

Chapter 27

"For we are God's masterpiece. He has created us anew in Christ Jesus, so we can do the good things he planned for us long ago."
~ Ephesians 2:10

"BALL THROUGH HOOP. It doesn't matter if it's ball off backboard through hoop or ball off rim to hoop. It can even be ball to alley through hoop but regardless of what road it travels, the end result has to be the same if we're going to win. Yes, defense is important but the team that scores the most points wins. Ball through hoop, it's just that simple."

****

SYMONE SAT IN HER car outside the Fairlawn Recreation Center. She smiled as she reminisced about her first day on Bodwen High school girls' varsity basketball team, Coach Mason's 'Ball through Hoop' preseason speech still resonating in her mind. She drummed her fingers on the steering wheel and waited anxiously for Chief's text. Chief already started practice with her AAU summer league team. She wanted to bring Symone in as a surprise so she asked Symone to wait for her cue.

Symone watched from her car window as young girls between the ages of ten and twelve years old funneled in and out of the recreation center doors. She smiled as she remembered that age, innocence border lining recklessness.

Symone heard the vibration of her phone as it danced on the dashboard. She checked her text message and saw that Chief was ready for her.

Symone stepped out of her car and flipped her hood onto her head. She wasn't sure if anyone would recognize her so she kept her head down until she entered the gym.

Chief stood before eleven impressionable faces when Symone slipped in. She removed her hood and immediately saw the animated pointing and heard gasps of surprise.

Chief looked behind her and smiled. "Most of you know my good friend Symone Holmes," she said to the team.

"Hi everybody," Symone said smiling.

"I saw you on TV," one player said with excitement oozing from every word. "You went number one."

"I sure did."

"So how come you not playing?" another player asked.

"I took the year off to take care of a sick family member but I still have to stay in shape so I'll be ready for next season and Coach Anderson told me this was the best team to workout with."

"You're training with us?"

"If you have room for one more player but you have to take it easy on me."

The look of delight on the players' faces brought a smile to Symone's face.

"So, who's the best player—" hands shot up before Symone could finish her sentence. Arguments broke out as players defended their playing abilities. "Whoa! Whoa!" Symone hushed the group. "All of you are right. This is AAU ball and only the best play AAU." A few of the girls nodded in agreement while others slapped each other five. "This age group is what?"

"Eleven and twelve year olds," Chief answered.

"Perfect age," Symone smiled. "By the time you get to high school, all of y'all will be the best players on your team. Keep your grades up and stay outta trouble and you can get a scholarship to play college ball then possibly end up in the league like me."

"That's where I'm tryna be," a player toward the front of the group said. She had an orange and white headband with matching wristbands, one she wore on her right leg just below her knee. She rested on her left knee, her right leg at a ninety-degree angle.

Symone could tell she was a guard by the way she moved the ball between her legs during the meeting. The determination in her eyes reminded Symone of herself when she was that age.

"Is that so?" Symone asked.

"Yep."

"You're gonna have to put in the work."

The young girl stood up and said, "I'm ready."

"She's just like you, Sy," Chief said. "Fearless."

Symone smiled. "Let's get started then."

Chief split the players up according to position. The point and shooting guards worked with Symone and the forwards and centers worked with Chief.

Symone practiced a variety of clear out and jab step techniques that would help the shooters get free for open jump shots. She also had them practice different shooting drills to help identify who were set shooters and who shot better on the move or off the dribble.

Symone noticed the girl with the orange and white headband had what basketball enthusiasts would call a pure stroke. Her shooting arm was perfectly aligned to the basket and the break in her wrist during the release of the ball sent the ball on an accurate path to the hoop. She had natural talent and Symone felt if taught by the right coach, she could be the next womens basketball prodigy coming out of Norfolk.

"Good work, ladies." Symone clapped as they completed the last drill. "Y'all tired yet?"

"I can go all night," the girl with the headband said.

"What's your name, youngin'?" Symone asked her.

"Wendy."

"Okay, Wendy. You stay with me, everybody else take a quick five minute water break."

Symone picked the basketball up from the floor and twirled it in her hands. "You gotta nice shot there, Wendy."

"Thanks. I work real hard at it. I shoot like, a hundred shots a day if I can."

"Yeah, I can tell you mostly practice set shots and off the dribble shots, right?" Wendy nodded. "You look very comfortable on the floor shooting those shots but you're struggling a bit with screen and rolls. You're fading back like this," Symone demonstrated Wendy's incorrect technique, "and that's why your shots are falling short. When you're coming off a screen, you still have to square your body to the basket after receiving the ball."

"I try to work on that but sometimes I don't have anybody to pass the ball to me."

"Use the wall," Symone suggested. "If you're in a gym like this, just throw the ball real hard at the wall at an angle so it'll bounce out in front of you." Symone demonstrated again. "See how I can curl to the ball just like I would curl off a screen to someone throwing me a pass?" Wendy nodded and listened intently. "You can use this drill to work on those moves and use the side walls for the same thing but for longer shots like three-pointers." Symone handed the ball to Wendy. "Try it."

Wendy took the ball and threw it at the wall behind the basket. The ball hit the wall and bounced too far in front of her. "Man!"

"Don't get frustrated," Symone said. "If the ball comes off the wall the wrong way, still play it like you're in a game. Either prepare yourself for another shot or bring it out as if you were starting the play over. Remember, you teammates won't always throw you that perfect pass so this helps you to think on your feet and keeps your head in the game."

"Okay cool."

Some of the players headed back from the break as Wendy worked on the drill. Symone began to pair the players in her mind to practice shooting off the screen and roll. Out the corner of her eye, Symone saw Chief having a heated discussion with what she assumed to be one of the parents.

"Um, go ahead and start some free throw drills and I'll be right back." Symone walked toward them and heard parts of the argument.

"I don't care who she is," the man said angrily. "I didn't pay good money to have my daughter working with some dyke. That's why we specifically asked her to be placed on *this* team."

"Is there a problem, Chief?" Symone asked calmly.

The man placed his hands on his hips and turned his back toward Symone.

Chief rolled her eyes when she saw he wasn't looking. "Mr. Jacobs is upset I didn't mention that you'll be working with the team, today."

Symone knew Mr. Jacobs didn't want to talk to her, which was the exact reason why she decided to force the issue. "Mr. Jacobs," she smiled politely, "I apologize for any inconvenience my presence has caused." Symone slid to her right to step into his field of vision. "But I'm taking the year off to take care of a family issue and since these girls are working to get where I'm at—"

"I understand all that," Mr. Jacobs said, still avoiding eye contact. "But I take my daughter's chance at a basketball career seriously."

"You don't think I can help those chances? I'm who your daughter wants to be."

Mr. Jacobs cut his eyes toward Symone and stated in a harsh tone, "My Wendy is NOT and will be nothing like you."

Symone's jaw tightened as she and Mr. Jacobs had a staring contest. She watched as his nose flared above his clean-shaven lip. His eyes narrowed as he leaned slightly forward, hoping to intimidate her with his six-four frame. Symone flashed a quick smile that caught him off guard and made him blink first.

"Mr. Jacobs, you're out of line," Chief said.

"It's okay, Chief," Symone assured her. "We wouldn't want Mr. Jacobs making any rash decisions that would cause him to put Wendy's future in jeopardy." Symone finally looked away and at Chief. "I'll catch up with you later and tell the girls I had fun."

Symone looked Mr. Jacobs over once more before heading to the exit.

Chapter 28

"He saved us, not because of the righteous things we had done, but because of his mercy. He washed away our sins, giving us a new birth and new life through the Holy Spirit." ~ Titus 3:5

BISHOP REED SAW ALL through bible study that Symone was unnerved. She was dressed in oversized basketball shorts and a zip-front hooded sweatshirt she wore on top of a sleeveless T-shirt. Bishop Reed assumed she was playing basketball and that was the reason for her tardiness. Symone sat in the back of the sanctuary and maneuvered between folding her arms across her chest and resting her forehead on the pew in front of her. She didn't have her bible nor was there any indication that she was using the bible application on her Smartphone. After the service was over and everyone exited, Bishop Reed sat down next to her in the pew.

"Long day?"

Symone leaned forward and rested her forearms on the pew in front of her. "You can say that."

"Do you want to talk about it?"

Symone stared past him and asked her own question, "Do you think being gay is wrong, Bishop?"

Bishop Reed hesitated. For the years he had been a spiritual counselor to Symone, she never once asked him that question. The fact that she was asking now, Bishop Reed knew he had to trend lightly to not break her spirit.

"What I think is not important." Symone smacked her lips and motioned to leave. Bishop Reed gently placed his hand on her arm to keep her seated. "Listen to me Symone. What I think is not important because we don't answer to man."

"But you're like his go between."

"My job as a pastor is to preach the gospel to the people. Once you have the information, God provides the wisdom for us to discern right from wrong."

"I try to live my life the best way I know how. Regardless of what people think, I'm a Christian first. Before I'm black, woman, gay, I live my life by the Word. I mean, yeah I screw up. I'm still human, a mortal but—" Symone pointed at his Bible, "I take that seriously. That's the only thing that—I dunno, Bishop. It's all I know. To even think that—"

"Nothing you can do will separate you from the love of God."

"I know but—to think me being gay makes this null and void—"

Bishop pointed at Symone and said, "Now that's your mistake right there."

"What?"

"Thinking this is based off what *you* do."

"Isn't it?"

"No. God's love for us has nothing to do with our performance. That's why He sent Jesus to be our Savior. We are righteous because of His love for us, not because of anything we did."

"So I can tell God I like girls and he'll still love me?"

"Of course. Where is all this coming from Symone?"

Symone thought about the comments Mr. Jacobs made at the recreation center. "I guess—I dunno—maybe I question whether God really loves me or not. I mean, you hear it so much on the TV and internet—everybody blaming gays for what's wrong with the world."

"You know that's not true."

"Do I?" Symone leaned back in the pew and sighed heavily. "Remember the last time we talked, you asked me why I hadn't thought about taking up or supporting any gay rights causes."

"Yes, you said you hadn't thought about it."

"Well, that's not entirely true," Symone confessed. "Truth is, my Christian beliefs keep me from embracing that world wholeheartedly. I don't even identify as lesbian but as a woman who loves women. I say it's because I don't want to be put into a labeled box but honestly, I—I'm not sure." Symone ran her hands over her face in frustration.

"I told you before, Symone. The only people who are ashamed or feel the need to hide are those who know they're doing something wrong."

"But that's just it. I don't feel my love for Regina is wrong but it's the world's reaction to our love that's got me hiding. I can't walk down the street holding her hand without someone turning their nose up or screaming obscenities at us. And let's not forget about me getting jumped and my truck being vandalized my freshman year of college." Symone said defensively, "I hide to protect myself and to protect Regina but I can't do it anymore. Even if I wanted to, I'm a celebrity now and everybody knows."

"God will not put more on you than you can bear." Bishop Reed saw Symone roll her eyes. "I know it's not something you want to hear but the truth never changes even though the circumstances do."

"I know," Symone sighed.

"And you can't judge your victory or love by the world's view."

"What do you mean by the world's view?"

Bishop Reed shifted his weight to keep his right leg from falling asleep. "The world views success by having a job or being rich. It views victory by championship rings or trophies and it views love based on feelings and physical contact. God's view is not like the worlds. God's view of success is based in us meditating on His Word and believing all that He has spoken will come to pass in our lives. God's view of victory is based in His unmerited favor that made us righteous despite our flaws and His view of love is evident in the sacrifice of His son Jesus and because of that sacrifice, because of Jesus blood, we can go to God and give every care we have in the world to Him."

They sat in silence as Symone allowed her mind to soak up Bishop Reed's words like a sponge.

"What if when it's all said and done, I was wrong and homosexuality really is a sin?" Symone asked.

"God will *still* love you."

"But will I go to hell?"

"Have you accepted Jesus as your Lord and savior?"

"Yeah."

"Then you are redeemed by the blood. I say again, it's not what you do but what you believe that saves you."

Symone smiled in relief. She was thankful for a pastor who dedicated his life to teaching truth regardless of his personal feelings about the matter.

"Thanks Bishop." Symone stood to her feet, stretched and headed for the door.

"And Symone," Bishop called out, "if God has truly blessed you with Regina, it'll become evident but you can't lose heart. God's love is unconditional and His love will always prevail."

Chapter 29

"But Christ has rescued us from the curse
pronounced by the law. When he was hung on
the cross, he took upon himself the curse for our
wrongdoing. For it is written in the Scriptures,
"Cursed is everyone who is hung on a tree."
Through Christ Jesus, God has blessed the
Gentiles with the same blessing he promised to
Abraham, so that we who are believers might
receive the promised Holy Spirit through faith."
~ Galatians 3:13-14

"OKAY, ONE MORE SET of leg lifts and we're done
for today."

Paula looked at Symone with disdain. It was
Monday, May 23rd, one week before Memorial Day
weekend. The day's workout had become number three
over six days. The training themselves had been going
well but there was no communication between Symone
and her mother. Symone tried to implement personal
conversations but if it wasn't about the workout, Paula
refused to respond.

"Don't look at me like that," Symone said.
"We've been doing good. You did some arm raises with
the eight ounce soup cans. We worked on your grip

strength and flexion in your hands, fingers and wrists. Now we're gonna get a little leg work in."

"I'm tired," Paula grumbled.

"This won't take long."

"I'm not doing them."

"Ma," Symone calmed herself down then said, "there won't even be any weights and you'll be sitting. Just straighten your leg out and then drop it."

Paula grunted more displeasure but did as asked. Symone had her do three sets of five with each leg.

"Good, good. Now one more."

"No!"

"Ma—"

"You said that was the last one."

"I know but I thought of one more. You don't have to stand and it's more of a stretch than an actual exercise."

"What?"

"I want you to bend your leg. I'm going to sit under you and you put your foot on my chest, right here." Symone tapped the upper part of her chest near her right shoulder. "Then I want you to push against me."

"Why?"

"It's gonna increase your flexibility and it also helps me to see how strong you're getting. Each week you should be able to push harder and this is the best way for me to tell without incorporating any weights."

Paula was a bit reluctant but she agreed to give it a try. Before they got started, Symone's phone rung. She looked at the Caller ID and saw it was Regina. Symone paused the 'ignore with message' feature on her phone and sent the automated text, *I'm busy. Will call you back.*

Before she could square herself in front of her mom, the incoming message buzzer on her phone sounded.

"On lunch, need to talk now."

"Ma, give me one second, okay." Symone stood to her feet and took the phone outside on the front porch to call Regina back.

"Hey baby, what's up?"

"So were you ever planning to tell me you didn't want me to come up there or was it just on me to get the hint?"

"Reggie—"

"I don't believe you Symone! You knew when you left you didn't want me to come with you."

"I told you that!"

"So why all the talk about you needed to go up there and assess things before—" Regina voice angered, "you only said that so I wouldn't put up a fight."

"No, see, that's not true."

"Really? So when did you talk with your brother about me coming up and staying awhile? Did you even mention it to him?" Symone remained silent. "I should've known." Regina said right before she hung up the phone.

"Freaking A," Symone grunted under her breath as she headed back into the house. She walked into the living room and found her mom and the electric scooter gone. "Cotton picking!" Symone yelled.

"Everything all right?"

Symone head snapped up and saw her father standing in the kitchen doorway eating a banana. "Yeah, I just—"

"Your mom again?"

"Actually no. It's Regina. She wanted to come here with me and I kinda lied to her so she wouldn't fight me on it."

"Oh." Frederick took another bite of his banana and said, "I don't mind if she comes—if that's what you're worried about."

"Nah, it's not that." Symone walked over to the sofa and sat on the floor in front of it. She pressed her back firmly against the front of the sofa, trying to crack her back. "I just—she wants so bad to be there for me, ya know. And I know that's not a bad thing but—I dunno, I just don't know how to let her."

"Sounds a lot like your brother," Frederick said as he walked into the living room and sat down in the folding chair adjacent to the sofa.

"Two peas in a pod, I guess," Symone said with a half smirk. "Truth is, she wants more than I'm able to give her."

"How so?"

Symone cocked her head toward her father. They've never had a conversation about her relationships. She barely mentioned anything about Regina to him except for her name. She felt awkward talking to him about their problems but she appreciated his concern and rewarded him by sharing, "Regina—she's real emotional. Not like, crying at the drop of a hat type emotional but she's big on talking 'bout feelings and stuff. I don't have that in me. Our family rarely expressed any outward emotion towards one another let alone talks about our feelings. I can't get her to understand she can't make me do something I don't know *how* to do."

"I guess that's my fault." Frederick lowered his head and stared down at the empty banana peel in his hands. "I tried my best to provide you and your brother with everything you'd need to live a good life. I fell short with the both of you."

"Dad—" Symone scooted to his side, "You can't blame yourself. You gave us the best of what you had. You couldn't give us what you didn't have just like I can't give Regina what I don't have but me and Ant turned out good. I mean, how many parents can say that *both* their kids are professional athletes. Not a whole lot and those who can say it are former professional athletes themselves."

"But you two are so distant—"

"It's just—it's apart of life sometimes but it has nothing to do with you. You gave us what we needed, food clothing, shelter and we have a strong foundation in Christ—"

"But not love," Frederick said sadly.

"Maybe not like we expected but of course love was there." Symone reassured him, "If you didn't love us you wouldn't've worked overtime and on weekends to provide for us. You wouldn't have cared so much when you thought Ant and Nicole were getting married so quickly and you definitely wouldn't have stood up to your family on my behalf. All of that shows me how much you love us."

"But you didn't know about that 'til a month ago when Ward told you."

Symone nodded in agreement. "But that goes back to not showing love." Symone saw that the statement didn't help to put her father at ease so she added, "It took some time to figure out but—it's like a generational curse in our family with this—need to not open up or let people in. And not just outsiders, anyone. Maybe somewhere someone was taught that it was weak to show emotion or express their feelings or maybe someone got hurt by letting someone get too close to them."

"It was an unspoken rule that the men in the family didn't show their feelings in front of their wives and children."

"But why though?"

"Men are the head of the household," Frederick stated as if he were reading from a script. "It's our duty to protect the family. Crying shows where we're weak and if your family thinks you're weak, they don't trust you to lead."

"That's crazy, dad."

Frederick sat back and shrugged his shoulders. "That's what my daddy told us and his daddy told him and his daddy told him."

"Like I said, generational curse." Symone shook her head. "We can't keep passing this down the line, dad. If nobody knew before, we know now that it's hurting the family. Having you—I dunno, just seeing you show something—" Symone fought back the tears, "it would've let me know you cared."

"But I did care, Symone. I do care."

"I know, I know but—there's something about showing it that backs up you saying it, ya know." Symone wiped her eyes and began to laugh. "Wow. I think that right there is what Regina's been trying to tell me. I finally get it."

"Then let it end with you." Symone looked into her father's watery eyes as he finished, "You see it and you understand the importance of it so let this generational curse end with you."

Chapter 30
(3 months later)

"My grace is all you need." ~ 2 Corinthians 12:9

KIDERA PULLED INTO HER apartment complex and parked her car next to Symone's. She was surprised to see that Symone was still at her place. If she came by, Symone always made it a point to leave before Kidera got home, even if she planned to stop by later.

Kidera entered her apartment and placed her keys on the table next to the door.

"I told you it's not safe to put your keys there," Symone yelled from the kitchen.

"Thanks dad," Kidera said sarcastically. She placed her book bag and purse in the chair and walked over to Symone with a Styrofoam container. "Surprised to see you still here."

"I just got here actually," Symone said as she rummaged through the refrigerator. "I was waiting in the car but figured you'd be here soon enough so why waste gas by burning the AC."

Kidera sat at the kitchen table and watched Symone sniff through food. "You cooking?"

"I would if you had something in here. When was the last time you went grocery shopping?"

Kidera offered her takeout plate. "Just have some of this."

Symone looked at the Styrofoam container suspiciously. "What is it?"

"¿Tienes hambre o no?"

Symone smacked her lips but grabbed a plate from the dish rack. Kidera shoveled half the chicken teriyaki with brown rice and vegetables onto the plate.

"So why are you just getting here?" Kidera asked.

Symone leaned her back against the counter and answered, "My mom had a doctor's appointment then I went to Waterside." Symone wasn't a fan of brown rice so she picked out the chicken and vegetables and ate them with her fingers.

"Uh oh." Kidera knew any time Symone went to Waterside, something was bothering her.

Symone sighed. "The doctor said the way we've been working with her over the past few months, she should've progressed further along than where she is."

"How so?"

"He did a bunch of random tests; mobility, strength, flexibility. He says she's getting better but after three months, there should be a lot more progress."

"Did he say what he thought was slowing her progression?"

Symone pointed to her head. "He said it's a mind thing. Either she doesn't realize how bad this stroke was and she didn't expect it to be this hard or she doesn't want to get better and she's doing just enough."

Kidera saw that Symone was hurting. She moved to comfort her but Symone pulled away.

"What did you used to tell me," Kidera began, "things don't work on our schedule but God's. You can't rush His progress, Symone."

Symone smiled softly. "Who would've thought, you actually learned something from me."

"I pay attention to you sometimes," Kidera smiled back.

For a brief moment, Symone was reminded of why she fell in love with Kidera. Outside of her beauty and sassiness, Kidera knew how to revert Symone's focus back to what was most important, her faith.

"You right though. I wanna see results now but maybe God has something bigger planned. I just have to remain patient and trust He has it all under control."

"That sounds more like the Symone I know."

Symone nodded to herself as she stared off into space. She snapped her head quickly to alert her senses. "Wow, I need sleep. You mind if I take a shower?"

Kidera shook her head no. As Symone headed to the back of the apartment, Kidera shouted, "Oh, my mom wanted me to tell you that you're invited to the family reunion Labor Day weekend."

Symone peeped her head back into the kitchen. "You told your mom I was in town?"

"You've been here three months. I'm surprised you haven't run into her yet."

"I don't know, Kid—"

"And she told me to tell you it's not an invite you can turn down," Kid said robbing Symone of the chance to decline.

Symone groaned under her breath as she walked back to the bathroom.

Kidera cleaned up the kitchen and decided to start on her homework. She poured herself a glass of iced tea and headed into the living room to study. Just as she was about to get started, she heard a phone ring. She jogged into the kitchen and found Symone's phone by the sink. The Caller ID read: Reggie.

Kidera heard the water running and figured Symone was in the shower. She decided against answering the phone and placed it on the kitchen counter. She moved toward the living room when Symone's phone rang again.

"Dammit!"

Kidera glanced at the Caller ID and saw it was her sister Kyra calling Symone.

"Mira hermanita."

"Kid?" Kyra answered surprised.

"Sí."

"Why are you answering Symone's phone?"

Kidera moved to the living room, placed her book bag and purse on the floor and sat down in the chair. "She's taking a shower. You want me to let her know you called?"

"Where are you?"

"I'm home."

"Why is Symone taking a shower, Kid?"

Kidera heard the insinuation lingering behind Kyra's tone. "It's not like that, Kyra okay. She stopped by to talk about her mom and asked if she could take a shower and a nap."

"A nap?"

Kidera opened her book bag and pulled out her Behavioral Analysis textbook. She placed it on the coffee table along with her notebook and pen.

Kidera leaned back into the chair cushion and let out a soft sigh. "Yes Kyra, a nap." Kidera thought it best to explain everything to avoid the long, drawn out conversation her older sister was sucking her into. "She doesn't get a lot of sleep at her brother's house because of the kids so every now and then she comes here to take a quick nap after working with her mom. And before you jump down my throat about this, I'm usually in class when she comes by. Today's the first time she's come by to shower and nap when I've been home."

"Does *Regina* know y'all hanging out?"

"I don't know. I don't ask her about her relationship with Regina. That's none of my business."

"Kid—"

"Kyra—"

There was a short pause before Kyra spoke. "Put Symone on the phone," she stated firmly.

"I just told you, she's in the shower."

"Llevale el cel al baño."

Kidera let out a loud sigh and took the phone to Symone in the bathroom as Kyra requested.

Kidera knocked on the door and opened it slightly. "Symone, Kyra's on the phone for you."

"Tell her I'm in the shower."

"I did."

Symone peeped her head around the shower curtain. Kidera had her left hand over her eyes and the phone extended out in her right hand.

Symone grudgingly took the phone. "Hello?"

"What the hell!"

"What?"

"You're at my sister's house in the show—er."

Symone rolled her eyes. "It's not that serious, Kyra."

"You do realize Kid is your EX-girlfriend." Kyra made sure to place extra emphasis on 'ex'.

"Yeah, from five years ago. We can't be friends?"

"Before you came back to V-A the two of you were barely talking but now y'all best buddies all of a sudden?"

"It's not all of a sudden and why is you worried about it? Nothing's going on. I talk to her just like I talk to you. Difference is, you respond by saying 'suck it up' or 'get over it' and she responds with just a little bit more compassion."

"It's sounding real suspect, Sy."

"Well, it's not," Symone tapped danced to the back of the tub, "cotton picking. Now the water's getting cold. I gotta go, Kyra."

"Symone—"

"Let it go, Kyra okay. I'm telling you, there's nothing going on with me and Kid."

"For your sake, I hope so," Kyra warned. "I really do hope so."

Chapter 31

"So humble yourselves under the mighty power of God, and at the right time he will lift you up in honor." ~ 1 Peter 5:6

SYMONE ROCKED BACK AND forth from her heels to her toes with her hands tucked in her armpits of her navy polo shirt. Regina's flight landed ten minutes earlier but no one exited the plane yet. Nathaniel latched onto Symone's leg tightly and made motor sounds with his mouth as he stood atop her black sneakers.

The first sign of passengers finally emerged from the gateway. Symone smiled softly when she saw Regina pulling her burgundy laptop bag across the carpet floor.

"Hey, baby." Symone reached down with her right hand and held Nathaniel steady as she hugged Regina with her left.

"Hey, Regina exhaled loudly.

"You should tired. The flight wasn't good."

"No, the flight was fine and thank you again for upgrading my ticket to first class."

"You don't have to thank me, Reggie. It's the least I could do."

"You mean since Sam bought the ticket in the first place?" Regina said with a hint of sarcasm.

"I told you I was gonna get it."

Regina rolled her eyes then glanced down into Nathaniel's big brown eyes. "Is this Nate Nate?" she asked surprised.

"Big ain't he?" Symone leaned down and scooped Nathaniel up in her arms. "You gonna say hi, Nate Nate?"

Nathaniel wrapped his tiny arms around Symone's neck and placed his head on her shoulders, never taking his eyes off Regina. The moisturizer from his soft, curly afro smeared a greasy smudge against Symone's cheek.

"He is so cute!" Regina shrieked. She held out her hand but Nathaniel resisted and clutched Symone's neck tighter.

"And shy," Symone replied. She peeked over his afro and said, "At least he's still looking at you. By now, he would've turned his head the other way."

"I guess that's a good sign."

Symone smiled and headed for the sign labeled 'Baggage Claim'. "Yeah, he must like you a little bit."

The wheels on Regina's laptop bag rolled over the brass bar as the carpet floor transitioned to vinyl. Nathaniel resumed his motor sounds, flowing harmoniously with the spinning of the wheels.

In the parking lot, Regina placed her suitcase in the back of the SUV since Nathaniel refused to set Symone free.

"Did you bring Nate Nate to keep me from fussing at you?" Regina asked as Symone strapped Nathaniel into his car seat.

"No—maybe."

Regina fanned her hand nonchalantly and headed to the passenger seat. "Don't worry, I'm over it now though I don't know how *anyone* could get over knowing their girlfriend didn't want to see them."

"See, there you go." Symone closed the back door and settled into the driver's seat. "I never said I didn't want to see you. I was gonna ask you to come up for the holiday weekend but Sam beat me to it."

"Humph—"

"What? I'm for real."

"Is that why you have plans with Chief tonight? Because you wanted me in town?"

"See, you got it all wrong again." Symone started the car and drove out the airport parking garage. "I don't wanna go to Chief's tonight—"

Regina squared her body to Symone and cut in sharply, "You don't want to go and watch basketball, the *playoffs*."

"No," Symone said quickly. "It's the WNBA playoffs. Why would I want to sit and watch other teams play for a spot in the championship when I never even got my chance to help my team make it this far? It would've been one thing to play and not make it but to never—"

Regina gently rubbed Symone's arm as Symone swallowed down the consequences in foregoing her rookie year as a professional athlete.

"So no," Symone resumed, "I don't wanna go tonight but Chief's a friend and she's throwing a party to support the game we all love and I'm gonna be happy for the teams that did make it. Even if I gotta fake it."

SYMONE EASED INTO ANTOINE'S driveway and found Briana standing on the front porch with her hands on her hips.

"I think you're in trouble," Regina said in a humorous tone.

"I swear that girl act just like her momma." Symone stepped out the SUV and smiled brightly at Briana. "Hey there, princess."

Briana stuck out her chin. "You left me," she pouted.

"Yes, yes I did," Symone admitted. "But my friend was waiting on me and I couldn't leave her all by herself."

Briana shifted to one side and saw Regina helping Nathaniel out of his car seat. She tapped her foot, flailed her arms and sighed a dramatically loud sigh.

"Are you really having a temper tantrum right now?" Symone asked surprised. "You know we don't do that."

"But I wanted to go," Briana whined.

Symone's heart broke at the sight of Briana's sad and disappointed face.

"Aww." Symone scooped Briana up in her arms and kissed her repeatedly on both cheeks until she began to laugh. "There's my happy big girl face. I promise next time I'll wait for you, okay?"

"Seal it with a kiss," Briana said.

Symone smiled widely. She always used that phrase with Briana when she was younger. It was their form of a secret handshake.

Briana braced herself as Symone took in a deep breath and attacked her cheeks with multiple kisses again. Symone suddenly stopped when she realized Regina was behind her holding Nathaniel's hand.

"Whoa! He let you touch him?"

"He put up a fight at first," Regina said. "Climbed out the chair all by himself but I told him he had to hold my hand to walk up the steps."

Symone smiled. "Did he give you his famous deep exaggerated sigh?"

"I thought it was just me."

"Nope, he does that." Symone laughed. "It's his way of saying, 'I guess' or 'I don't want to but I'll do it'."

Regina followed Symone into the house. Both children released from their grips and darted toward the kitchen.

"Smells like someone's cooking," Symone said as the aroma of chicken and spices teased her nose.

"Nikki's making chicken tacos." Antoine stood up from the sofa and walked toward Regina. "Long time no see, stranger," he said with a hug.

"Blame your sister," Regina replied.

"Oh, I have."

"And that's why we're not staying," Symone interjected with a quaint smile.

"So, you're just going to do a drive-by drop off with my son?"

Regina pointed to the kitchen before heading in that direction. Symone acknowledged her excusal with a nod.

"She just got off a plane, Ant. She's gonna need rest before putting in a full day with Bri and Nate."

"You right about that."

"She's in town through the weekend so we'll stop back by. I know dad wanna do lunch or something so—"

Regina reentered the living room nibbling on a soft shell taco.

"Greedy," Symone teased.

"Says the one who wants a bite."

"As long as you know."

Regina tempted Symone with the taco playfully but soon gave in and fed her a few bites.

"Yeah, that's on point right there." Symone nodded in approval.

"You talking like my wife doesn't know how to cook."

"Honestly Ant, I wasn't sure. All that hummus and tofu—" Symone shuddered at the thought, "not the business."

Antoine peeked over his shoulder and tipped his head in agreement.

"It was good seeing you again, Regina." His voice was louder than usual as he tried to hide the fact the previous conversation included unpleasant gossip.

Regina shook her head at the sister-brother tandem. "You two are a mess." She hugged Antoine one last time then followed Symone out the door.

"You're taking me to Sam's now, right?"

"I thought you might wanna go to the hotel and rest up first."

"Um, no. I'll hang with Sam a bit. Kyra's probably going to Chief's party too so my best friend and I might make tonight our own girls night out."

Symone laughed softly and started the SUV. "I can see it now. You and Sam up in the strip club with a handful of ones."

"Who's to say *we'll* be handing out the ones," Regina said with a devilish smile. "Maybe we'll be collecting them. I do have a few skills."

"Maybe we should go by the hotel so you can practice your routine first."

"Practice does make perfect," Regina said seductively.

"Girl, you keep talking like that, neither one of us is going anywhere tonight!"

Chapter 32

"So let's not get tired of doing what is good. At just the right time we will reap a harvest of blessing if we don't give up." ~ Galatians 6:9

"YOU HAVE NO IDEA how bad it's hurting me to be here right now."

Chief smiled at Symone despite the negative comment. "See it as motivation," Chief said. She wrapped her arm around Symone's shoulders and led her into the house. "Just in case you were getting a little *too* comfortable with you time off."

The right corner of Symone's mouth curled up as she gave Chief her patented 'yeah right' look.

Purple and black, the official team colors of the WNBA team Sacramento Monarchs, invaded Chief's spacious two-bedroom apartment. It was opening night of the WNBA playoffs and Chief was hosting the party for the first round. Most of the guests were women basketball players from local colleges or former players who still loved the game. The rest were family and friends who attended any party with food and drinks.

"Monarchs, Chief. Really?" Symone said.

"This house supports the local players. Ticha Penicheiro's a graduate of ODU so she's reppin' Norfolk." Chief patted Symone on the back and joked, "Don't worry. You take Charlotte to the playoffs and I'll have my interior designer come in and make the color change."

Symone quickly realized this was the first time she hung out with most of her old schoolmates since she'd been back to Virginia. After the incident with some of the parent's of Chief's AAU team three months ago, Symone stayed away from the recreation center. Her main focus in returning to Norfolk was to help her mom so she made that priority number one. Her second priority was to make sure she wouldn't lose her sanity in the process.

Many of the guests offered their sympathy to Symone in relation to her mother's illness while others congratulated her in making it to the league.

"We can't wait to see you on the court," Trenise, a former Bodwen High player said.

Her friend Gloria added, "It'll be sweet to have two Norfolk women basketball players, you and Ticha, with a chance to win a WNBA championship title!"

"She's gotta get past LA first," Symone said. "Lisa Leslie's a beast and she wants ring number three."

"Yo, Sy!"

Symone looked up and saw Kyra waving her over. Symone excused herself from the two women and made her way to her.

"What's up?" Symone asked.

"Just making sure you're good."

"Yeah, I'm good." Symone shrugged her shoulders. "Can't be mad. I chose this but I can't lie, I miss playing like crazy. That's why I haven't watched any games all season. Keep myself from spasing out or crying or something."

"I hear you." Kyra took a swig of her beer and asked directly, "So what you doing with Kid?"

Symone rolled her eyes and grunted. She had a feeling the topic was not closed for further discussion. "I told you, between dealing with my mom and Ant's family, I needed a break. I was gonna get a hotel room but Kid suggested I just stop by her place and crash when I need to."

"So you're staying there."

"No, I'm staying at Ant's but after I work with my mom, sometimes I go to Kid's to take a nap while she's in class."

"And why you can't go back to Antoine's to take a nap?"

"Because Nicole is a stay at home mom which means the kids are there with her all day. There is no taking a nap there."

Kidera took another sip and shook her head. "Just don't sound right."

"What you talking about? My brother has two kids who are out of school for the summer so they're at the house all day long. I can't deal with all that noise, Kyra especially after getting the cold shoulder from my moms for two to three hours out the day. Not to mention the kids don't go to bed 'til ten, eleven o'clock then turn around and wake up at five or six in the morning. I just needed a place to clear my head and to get some rest."

"Regina know?" Kyra asked as though she already knew the answer to the question.

"There's nothing to tell."

"Like I said, suspect."

Symone shifted her weight from her right foot to her left. She was agitated with Kyra's accusations.

"Look, there couldn't be nothing between me and your sister anyway. Regardless of whatever situation I *might've* created back then, she still cheated on me and I could never trust her with my heart again." Symone turned and faced Kyra, almost challenging her. "And why would I put Reggie through something like that knowing how it feels to have someone you love step out on you, huh?"

"Hey now," Chief interrupted after seeing the tension increase between the two from across the room. "Everybody playing nice over here?"

"We good," Kyra said with a sly smile. "Just making sure Symone's got her priorities in check."

Chief knew there was more to the story by the way Symone glared at Kyra. It made sense to end things now before they had a chance to get out of hand.

"Symone," Chief began, "why don't you come check out the game. Break down and analyze what you see. Maybe school some of those college girls in there who're trying to get where you're at."

Symone shook her head at Kyra and followed Chief into the living room.

"What's up with you two?" Chief asked.

"It's nothing."

Chief resisted the temptation to pry deeper. More pressing matters needed to be addressed. "Aye, I wanted to apologize for Wendy's dad—"

"Forget about it, Chief."

"Nah, he wasn't right. My bad in taking so long but you haven't been around—"

"I just been trying to focus more on my mom. Get her right, ya know."

"I feel you."

"But Wendy's got skills," Symone replied. "She's gonna be nice if her dad doesn't ruin it for her."

Chief grunted. "I think he's noticed Wendy's showing 'tendencies' and he's trying to keep her on lockdown."

"Oh, she's a lil' stud in the making," Symone stated plainly. "And if some chick don't test her out in high school, she's definitely gonna have a few break her in when she gets to college and there ain't nothing *dad* can do about that."

Chapter 33

"And I am certain that God, who began the
good work within you, will continue his work
until it is finally finished on the day when
Christ Jesus returns." ~ Philippians 1:6

SYMONE TOOK SHORT QUICK breaths as she
helped Regina unload the car. It was a beautiful
September afternoon, the temperature in the mid-
seventies. The perfect weather for a Labor Day family
reunion in the park.

Symone and Regina arrived at the parking lot of
Mount Trashmore Park in Virginia Beach.

"Are you sure Kidera's family is all right with me
showing up?" Regina asked Symone as they carried the
dishes toward the reserved picnic gazebo.

"Shoot, I'm not sure if they're okay with *me*
showing up." Regina looked at Symone in disbelief. "I'm
kidding," Symone said smiling.

Regina was not amused. "That's not funny. I just
want to make sure—"

"¡Valgame! Symone, Symone! ¡No puedo creer
que eres tu!" Kidera's mother cried tears of joy as she
hugged and kissed Symone.

Regina stepped back and watched in complete
shock. Never had she seen someone display such open

affection toward Symone nor had she seen Symone willingly accept any.

"¡Te he extrañado tanto! ¡Vena ca, dame una abraza!" Kidera's mother stayed true to her heritage, only speaking in her native language.

Kidera emerged from the back of the gazebo to save Symone from her mother's love. "Ma, la vas a hacer dejar caer la comida."

Symone smiled at the mother-daughter interaction. "Mrs. Maria," Symone began, "let me put the food down and I'll give you all the hugs and kisses you can stand."

Symone sat the dishes down on the fold out table set up outside the gazebo. Once her arms were free, more of Kidera's family swarmed around her like a pack of honeybees.

"Amazing isn't it?" Kidera said to Regina. "It's like they never missed a beat."

"I see."

Kidera saw that Regina felt out of place so she offered her friendship. "Why don't you put the plates down anywhere and I'll introduce you to everybody. Symone will probably be tied up for a while."

Regina felt very uncomfortable around Kidera's family without Symone by her side. She was surprised Kidera was so nice to her but she was appreciative. However, having the ex-girlfriend introduce her as Symone's girlfriend to the ex-girlfriend's family did not add any necessary comfort to the niceness.

"Reggie!" Symone called. "I'm so sorry, baby," she said as she approached Regina. "I didn't know they were gonna come at me like gang busters."

"You're still very popular with Kid's family."

"Yeah, um, they stepped up big time when things got rough with my family. Mrs. Maria and Edwin, Kid and Kyra's stepdad, became like second parents to me.

That's why the breakup with Kid was so hard for me back then. I felt like I lost a family again."

"I can tell they've really missed you."

"Yeah." Symone felt weird talking to Regina about her attachment to Kidera's family so she shifted the focus of the conversation to the food.

"You ready to eat?"

"Am I," Regina said with a half-hearted smile.

Symone grabbed her by the hand and led her to the Spanish cuisine.

Symone's eyes widened and her mouth watered at the spread of food before her. Traditional Spanish dishes like pernil and arroz con gandules were customary at every Fuentes gathering. An assortment of pasteles including guinero and yuca caused the hunger pains in Symone's stomach to voice their delight.

"Mrs. Maria, guinero lleno de bananas o plantains?" Symone asked in Spanglish.

"Platanos."

Symone looked at Mrs. Maria curiously, not sure if she understood what was asked.

"Kid," Symone called, "Ask your mom if the guinero is made with bananas or plantains."

"Why don't you ask her yourself?"

"I did but she said platanos and I know that both bananas and plantains are called platanos in Spanish."

"Just ask her a different way."

Symone huffed. "Just ask her for me. You know I don't like plantains."

"You don't speak fluent Spanish anymore?" Kidera asked sarcastically.

Symone rolled her eyes. "I still listen to Spanish radio to try and stay up with it but it's hard when you don't speak it everyday. I guess I've gotten rusty these past four years."

"Um hmm."

Kidera asked her mother and found out the pasteles de guinero were made with bananas. Symone smiled in satisfaction as she added them to her plate.

"Have you heard from Kyra?" Regina asked Symone.

"Naw, I haven't."

"I'm texting her now," Kidera replied with her phone in her hand. "I want to make sure she brings the music. They're on their way." Without thinking, Kidera used her hip to bump Symone's. "You still know how to Bachata, sí?"

"Yeah," the corner of Symone's lip curled up into a half crescent smile, "but I'm only dancing with your Uncle Raymond. The rest of y'all don't know how to keep your hands in the safe zone."

"Don't point at me." Kidera laughed. "You were always the one trying to make love on the dance floor."

Symone shuffled her feet to the Salsa music already blaring from someone's portable stereo. Regina blushed as Symone swayed her hips in an attempt to get her to dance. Even though Symone's playful antics where a welcoming surprise, Regina was still hesitant to loosen up amongst the unfamiliar group.

Members from Kidera's family saw Symone dancing and joined in. The ease in which Symone settled into the family atmosphere disturbed Regina more than she was willing to let on.

Regina crossed her arms and anxiously rocked back and forth on her boot heel. She glanced toward the parking lot and saw Kyra's car pull in.

"Thank god." Regina exhaled as she headed in that direction.

After a few more dance moves with Mrs. Maria, Symone spotted Kyra's car in the parking lot but the heated discussion between Regina and Samantha drew her attention.

What are they arguing about now? Symone thought as she walked toward them.

"Hey, is everything all right?" Symone asked Regina without speaking to Samantha or Kyra.

"I'm fine, Symone."

"No she's not," Samantha stated. "She wants me to take her back to the hotel."

"What? Why?"

"You tell us, dawg," Kyra said in a frustrated tone.

Symone ignored the comment and looked to Regina for answers.

"I don't feel like talking about it."

Symone sensed obvious tension in Regina's voice. "Talk about what? I don't even know what's wrong?"

"Maybe you and Kid, for one," Kyra said.

Symone's eyes shot daggers in Kyra's direction but Kyra shrugged them off like they were plastic toy knives.

"Don't start, Kyra," Symone warned.

"You already started it, having sleepovers with your ex. Hell, I ain't even bold enough to try that shit."

Symone's face flushed with anger at Kyra putting her on the spot in Regina's presence. Kyra recognized the look and replied, "Don't worry. I ain't putting you on front street. Regina already knows about your creeping."

The punch happened so quickly, it caught everyone off guard, even Symone. She didn't realize she hit Kyra until she saw Kyra down on all fours, tiny drops of blood falling from her cut lip.

Kyra rolled over onto her backside and laughed. Samantha quickly ran to her aid.

Kyra licked at the fresh cut and said, "And here I thought you didn't have it in you."

"Are you crazy!" Samantha yelled. "What did you hit her for?"

Symone tried to shake off the sting from her knuckles as she replied, "'Cause she running her mouth to Reggie about stuff that ain't even true!"

"*I* told her, Symone."

Symone looked at Samantha confused. "How you tell her? I don't even talk to you."

"I heard you and Kyra talking that time you were taking a shower at Kid's but you know what, it doesn't matter. If you weren't doing anything you wouldn't've been trying to hide it from Regina."

"Wow." Kidera walked up behind Regina moments earlier and heard the entire conversation. She was amazed at how everything had been blown out of proportion.

"I wasn't hiding anything, Sam." Symone turned back to Regina. "She hears one half of a conversation, draws an assumption and this is what we get."

"Wait a minute now," Kyra stood to her feet, "don't make it seem like Sam's in the wrong. You're the one who didn't tell Regina what was going on—"

"'Cause there's nothing going on!" Symone shouted. She turned to Regina again and repeated more calmly, "There's nothing going on, I promise you."

"Yeah, they just friends," Kyra said mockingly. "Like the old Biz Markie song."

"Ugh!" Symone screamed and kicked the side of Kyra's car. "What is wrong with you!" She stormed at Kyra and pinned her up against the trunk of the car.

Samantha and Regina moved to help but Kyra held her hand up to stop them.

"Do you gotta vendetta against me or something?" Symone asked angrily. "You mad 'cause I made it in the league and you didn't? You supposed to be my dawg. Do you *not* want me to be happy?"

"I want you to do better," Kyra said smugly. She brushed Symone's hands off her shirt and took a few steps forward which made Symone step back. "You blame everybody else for what's wrong in your life; your mom, Kid, me. Take some fucking responsibility for the decisions *you* made. And it you can't do that then no, you don't deserve to be happy. You haven't earned the right to be."

Symone pushed away from Kyra and headed into the park opposite the family gathering. She was finished talking to Kyra. Symone didn't believe one word that was said and after their many years of friendship, it hurt her to know Kyra felt that way about her.

"Symone!" Regina called after her. "Symone!"

"She's a piece of work, Reggie," Symone said still moving at a quick pace. "She wanna hate on *me*? Judge *me*?"

"Symone where are you going?"

"I need to hit something!"

"There's nothing out here to hit."

Symone walked to the nearest trashcan. She picked it up with both hands, held it over her head and slammed it to the ground as hard as she could.

"Symone!" Regina placed her hand on Symone's shoulder.

Symone turned and stared at Regina with tears in her eyes. "Baby, I'm telling you—"

"Listen to me," Regina interrupted. She gently grabbed Symone by both sides of her face and kissed her softly on the lips to calm her down. "I believe you, okay. I know you wouldn't hurt me like that. Not after knowing what it feels like to have someone you love cheat on you."

"So why you tell Sam you wanted to go back to the hotel?"

"I—" Regina released Symone's face and stared past her to the family reunion site. "We've been together four years and I've never, I mean *never* seen you be so— open and—carefree like you are with Kid's family. I've tried to get you involved with my family like this but you've always been so—reserved, distant. The laughing, joking around, and dancing you did today—you haven't seen these people in over four years and yet it doesn't seem like it."

"So wait, you're mad because—"

"I'm not mad, Symone. I'm just—confused. What is it about Kid and her family that—brings out the best in you?"

"The best?" Symone wanted to take offense to the statement but knew it wasn't the right time. Her relationship with Kidera's family had affected Regina and she needed to address that issue first.

"I told you, Reggie. Kid's family became a second family to me after mine disowned me. I didn't know what to expect coming here today especially when I haven't talked to any of them since me and Kid broke up. I dunno but—just them still being the same, ya know, in not judging or holding grudges after all these years—"

"My family never judged you."

"I know." Symone took Regina by the hands and led her to the nearest picnic table to sit. "But it takes time. I didn't immediately connect with Kid's family either. Maybe it's taking longer with your family because they're not local and I don't have the opportunity to bond with them on a daily basis like I did with Kid's family."

"Or maybe you're not trying."

"Reggie—"

"No, I'm serious, Symone. You're afraid because you thought you lost two families, your own and Kid's. I understand that, I do but I'm afraid that you reconnecting with Kid's family is going to keep you from trying harder with mine. You got what you want right here—"

Symone wiped the tears that fell upon Regina's cheeks. "Don't think like that, Reggie. See this as a good thing." Regina looked at Symone doubtfully. "No, think about it," Symone began, "You thought I didn't have this in me at all. Shoot, so did I. Now we know I do. I now know what it is you need from me 'cause I have something to relate it to."

"Symone—"

"Me and my dad talked about it already," Symone cut in. "We talked about breaking generational curses. I don't wanna pass this—emotionless state down to our kids. I don't want our kids to be without hugs and kisses and 'I love you's' from me. I want them to not just know they're loved but feel that they're loved. I didn't think I could give you that but now I know I can." Symone hugged Regina tightly and replied, "This is something we can build on together. I know I can do this now because it's already in me. It's been in me the whole time. This gathering just helped ignite it."

Chapter 34

"God's way is perfect. All the LORD's promises prove true. He is a shield for all who look to him for protection." ~ Psalms 18:30

SYMONE SAT AT THE kitchen table surfing the internet on her laptop computer. She repeatedly glanced at the phone impatiently waiting for Regina's call to say that she landed.

"I still don't get why she had to leave," Antoine said. It was as though he had eyes in the back of his head watching Symone from the living room.

"I told you, her boss called last night and said they just gotta major contract. Everybody's gotta report to work tomorrow."

"But it's Labor Day. Her boss couldn't wait one more day?"

"I guess not. They're a small company, Ant. A big enough project could help them expand."

"Why is she working anyway?"

"Duh, because she wants to."

Antoine grabbed a decorative pillow from the sofa and flung it over his head in Symone's direction. He missed by a few feet.

"What I meant was why is she working for someone else. She should be working for herself, making her own hours."

"Yeah, then I would never see her."

"You would if she worked from home."

"Says the man who sends his pregnant wife to *Chucky Cheese* with two small children so he can play games on the computer."

"I'm making a video for one of my songs."

Symone glanced at her phone again. No call yet.

Symone grunted, left the kitchen and walked into the living room where Antoine had his laptop. She glanced over his shoulder from behind the sofa and watched him piece different video clips into a four-minute music video.

"See."

"Yeah, yeah." With the house empty, Symone thought it was a good time to ask Antoine his true feelings about her relationship with Regina. "Can I ask you something, Ant?"

"Sure. What's up?"

"What do you think about me and Regina?"

"What?"

"You heard me."

Antoine looked up behind him to see if Symone was serious. She was.

"I don't know." He shrugged. "I've only met her a few times. She seems nice."

"But what do you think about us together?"

Antoine said with a sly smile, "You're my sister. I don't want to think of y'all together."

"You know what I mean." Symone popped him in the back of the head.

Antoine laughed then shrugged his shoulders again. "If you're asking from the standpoint that both of you are women, I don't care. Shoot, if I was a woman I would be a lesbian too."

"You say that 'cause you're thinking like a man."

"What do you expect?"

Symone thought for a moment then asked, "What if ten years from now, Brianna came home with a girlfriend?"

"I can't tell you how'd I feel but I'd still love her just like I still love you. Why are you asking?"

"I love Regina and I want to have with her what you and Nicole have. I want to marry her."

"Oh."

Symone was taken aback by Antoine's immediate reaction. "Oh? What does 'oh' mean?"

Antoine let out a deep sigh. He sat his laptop next to him on the sofa and turned to face Symone.

"Marrying her, Sy? I don't know—"

"See, I knew—"

"All I'm saying is, I don't know. I'm still a man of God and—"

"So, you're saying you're okay with me and Regina being together as long as we don't get married. Isn't that backwards?" Symone felt her tone rising but she didn't care. "Isn't marriage supposed to be the commitment we make to that one person before God, honoring God in that love?"

Antoine pursed his lips and tilted his head from side to side. "Like I said, I don't know. I don't think I would've had a second thought about it if it wasn't for you. I can only tell you what I believe."

"Would you come though?"

"You know I would. If you believe Regina is who God wants you to spend your life with then I'll back you on that. If it changes and it ends up being someone else, man or woman, I'll support you in that too. That's what families," Antoine paused and restated, "that's what families are *supposed* to do." Antoine saw Symone was still upset by his discontent so he added, "Your love for Regina is between you, her and God. I have no place to judge that."

"See, when people say that, they're always referring to bad stuff they've done. You can't compare my love for Regina with some trouble you got into in the past."

Antoine opened his mouth to speak but stopped. Even though he didn't mean to insult her, Symone was right. When he said he had no place to judge, he was saying it from a place where he was comparing his wrongdoings to their love. However, there was something Antoine could offer to hopefully bring Symone some comfort.

Antoine stood up, walked to the window and looked outside. He wanted to make sure Nicole had not returned with the kids yet.

"I'm going to tell you something I've never told anyone *and* you have to promise that it stays between us."

"O-kay," Symone said nervously. She sat down on the back of the sofa while Antoine sat on the window seal.

Antoine let out a loud sigh. "When I was in college, I had a homeboy who was madly in love with this woman. They got married and about a year into the marriage, they decided to start working on their family. After six months of trying with no success, they went to a fertility doctor and found out he was sterile. It really put a strain on their marriage to the point he thought she was going to divorce him. He asked me if I would donate my sperm so they could have a baby. I told him that I would want to be in the child's life somehow so he said I could be the godfather and I was good with that." Antoine moved away from the window and started pacing the living room floor. "Well, I go deliver my goods and a week later, my homeboy tells me his wife has fibroids and they can't impregnate her until the fibroids shrink or are removed. The wife didn't want to wait the three months to take the medicine to shrink the fibroids so they opted for a surgery to remove them. To make a long story short, they ended up finding more fibroids once they cut her open and by the time they removed them all, there wasn't enough of her uterus to put back together so she ended up having a hysterectomy. They were heartbroken of course but all I could think was, my boys are still in the system where anybody can get to them now." Tears began to weld in Antoine's eyes. "I could have a kid out there somewhere who doesn't know me and who *I* don't know."

Symone watch him in awe. The only time she ever saw Antoine cry was when their grandmother passed away. To know his good intentions to help a friend had left him feeling helpless in not knowing if he had other children out in the world saddened her.

"You couldn't go back and have them destroy what you donated?"

Antoine shook his head. "When I signed the release form, it gave my homeboy and his wife rights over my sperm. He said they were gonna find a surrogate and try to have a baby that way but after I left school for the NBA, we lost touch. He moved and disconnected his number. I tried calling mutual friends in North Carolina but no one knew where they relocated. It's like they just fell off the face of the earth and my kid could be with them."

"You can't beat yourself up about that, Ant."

"Why not? If I was more worried about my responsibilities instead of going pro—"

"But it not your responsibility anymore. if they had a child, it's on them to take care of it."

Antoine stopped pacing and faced Symone. With a serious look on his face he said, "What happens when that child grows up and finds out Heather and Cliff aren't his biological parents. What if that child comes looking for me, wanting to know who I am? What do I say when they ask why haven't I been in their life all these years. What do I tell Nicole?"

"Wait, she doesn't know?" Symone asked surprised.

"We only been dating about six months when all this happened. I talked to her about it and she didn't want me to do it. She didn't want to be with someone who had illegitimate children. Cliff was like a brother to me and I really felt God placed it on my heart to help them so I did it without her knowing."

"Wow, and I thought I was dealing with some stuff."

"I guess we both been scratching at old scars," Antoine said as he walked over to her, "keeping them from healing right."

Symone thought about her conversation with her dad in ending the generational curse. "Let's make a promise," she began. "No more handling hard times on our own. We're family and we need to learn to depend on each other when we feel we can't talk to anyone else."

"You're right. I can't tell you how bad that's been eating at me."

Symone leaned forward and poked him in his stomach like the Pillsbury doughboy. "That's probably what ate away your six-pack," she joked.

Antoine laughed. "Probably." He smiled at Symone and said, "All right. From here on out, it doesn't matter how bad something gets and regardless of whether the other one can fix it or not, I call you, you call me. No more doing it alone."

"Bet."

Symone's phone chimed and she rushed to check the text message.

"She made it?" Antoine asked.

Symone smiled, "Yeah, she's home."

Chapter 35

"Commit everything you do to the LORD.
Trust him, and he will help you."
~ Psalms 37:5

IT WAS A COLD Fall day in October and Symone could not believe how much her life had changed since draft day. Instead of fulfilling her dreams of playing in the WNBA, she wound up back in Virginia trying to rehabilitate her resentful mother. The thought alone drained her but her mother's continued lack of progress left her feeling defeated.

Symone continued to see spiritual counseling from Bishop Reed and something he said when she visited him after the incident at Mount Trashmore stuck with her.

It's possible you forced yourself upon this situation. You want your mother well but you came to Virginia in hopes of changing her heart but we can't change people, only God can.

Symone wondered if he was right. Others were willing to help or she and Antoine could've pitched in to hire a certified physical therapist, someone who could've gotten her mother to respond better than what she had done. Had her sacrifice in coming to Virginia been her own doing and not God's? Did she try to force God's hand in fixing their relationship or did she not trust Him anymore due to lack of results from the past?

The frustration mounted upon Symone's shoulders weighed her down and she wasn't sure of how to handle it. She hoped starting the day with a daily devotional would sooth her soul. To her surprise, the message talked about unforgiveness being a barrier to healing.

"There's gotta be something to this unforgiveness, Lord," Symone said aloud. "You've had me circle around this too many times for it not to mean something." Symone thought for a moment then knew what she had to do. "She's not going to like this but it's time to conquer this demon head on."

While Symone drove to her parents' house, she placed a call to her brother at his studio.

"What's up sis?" Antoine answered.

"I need you to come to mom and dad's ASAP."

Symone immediately heard papers shuffling and keys jiggling on the other end of the phone. "Why? Did something happen?"

"No. Nothing's been happening and that's the problem."

"What you have in mind?"

"It's time to get violent with it."

Symone explained her plan to Antoine who listened intently. He advised her to wait until he arrived before getting started. She agreed. She pulled into her parents' driveway and waited for Antoine.

"You sure you want to do it like this?" Antoine asked when he arrived.

"I don't see no other option. We've tried everything else."

"You told dad yet?"

"Nope. Figured might as well let it be a surprise to him, too."

Frederick had already started training with Paula in the living room when Symone and Antoine arrived.

"Hey you two," Frederick said. "I thought I'd get your mom started, have her warmed up for you."

Symone looked at Antoine for reassurance. He nodded. Symone faced her parents and said, "We want to try something different today."

"Oh?"

"We want to do a prayer circle."

Frederick sat back as Antoine explained, "We think something might be blocking mom's healing so we want to pray and ask God to reveal anything that's hindering her breakthrough."

"All right." Frederick stepped aside and made room for Paula to steer the electric scooter to the middle of the living room floor.

Symone stepped in between her father and Antoine and grabbed their hands. Paula was in between the two men on the opposite side, which put her directly across from Symone. Everyone bowed their heads. Antoine gently squeezed Symone's hand.

Symone peeked out the corner of her eye at him, drew in a deep breath and began, "Father God, we thank you for bringing us here together today. We thank you for your sovereign power and the blood of your son Jesus that has made us righteous through no part of our own. We come to you today declaring the finished work of healing over our mother and wife—well, ex-wife." Antoine tugged at Symone's hand. Symone tugged his back. "We know her healing has already been made available to her through the blood Jesus shed from the stripes on his back. But we also know the devil manipulates us into thinking we're not healed or uses circumstances in our lives to take our eyes off you, causing us to block the healing transfer from the spirit to our physical bodies. Your word tells us in Mark 11:25 that we must forgive anyone we're holding a grudge against so we can receive your forgiveness and your healing is in line with that. So we pray right now Father in the name of Jesus that you bring to light the unforgiveness and resentment she's been harboring that's been blocking her faith from accessing your healing power." Symone heard shuffling in her mother's directions but she kept her eyes closed and continued, "Don't allow the devil to hold her hostage to her own vices any longer."

The sound of the electric scooter powering up caused Symone to stop and open her eyes.

"She's not finished, ma," Antoine said.

"You let her come in here and talk to me like this," Paula stammered. "How dare you!"

Paula punched the joystick forward but Symone stepped in her path, preventing her from motoring off.

"We can't keep doing this, ma."

"Move."

"Do you wanna die 'cause that's what the devil's doing. He's killing you slowly from the inside out."

Paula was furious. She felt blindsided by the prayer circle and she didn't want to deal with anyone anymore. She tried to pull the joystick backward to move her scooter in reverse but her hand kept slipping off the handle.

"I'm sorry, okay," Symone said shamefully. "I'm sorry me being gay hurts you but it doesn't change who I am. I'm still that soft-spoken shy little girl who everyone takes a liking to. I'm still that same mischievous adolescent who can smile her way out of trouble. I'm still the same generous soul who puts others before myself even when it means I have to sacrifice something I love to do it." Symone knelt down in front of the scooter with tears in her eyes and cried, "But most of all, I'm still your daughter and I need my momma. I'm hurting not having you apart of my life."

Paula's face was as hard as a stone statue. "You try and trick me."

"What? I didn't—"

"You come here and you try and trick me." Paula finally got a grip on the joystick to put the scooter in reverse. "No more training." She maneuvered the scooter around Symone and stated, "Leave me alone forever."

"Why can't we go back to the way things were, ma? Jesus loves me for who I am. Why can't you?"

Paula's eyes narrowed and with a cold glare, she stated harshly, "I'm not Jesus."

"Paula!" Frederick followed her down the hall to the bedroom.

Symone didn't wait around for Antoine to try to console her. Neither he nor anyone could offer the right words to mend the brokenness in her heart.

Chapter 36

"I have fought the good fight, I have finished
the race, and I have remained faithful."
~ 2 Timothy 4:7

THE URGENT BANGING ON the door startled
Kidera. She used the peephole to see who was causing the
commotion.

"Symone?" Kidera said softly to herself.

As soon as Kidera opened the door, she could tell
something was wrong. Symone's eyes were red and her
cheeks were flushed. Kidera knew right away that Symone
had been crying.

"What happened?" Kidera asked.

Symone opened her mouth to speak by no words
came out. Instead, the tears began to flow again. Kidera
wrapped her arms around Symone's shoulders and led her
into the apartment. They sat down on the loveseat and
Symone continued to cry in Kidera's arms.

Symone finally composed herself and breathed a
sigh of relief.

"Are you ready to talk about what's going on?"
Kidera asked.

Symone nodded. She scooted toward the far end
of the loveseat then laid her head in Kidera's lap. The
action surprised Kidera but she did not object or resist.

"I'm going back to Charlotte," Symone said.

"Already?"

"Yeah, I just—my mom's not gonna get better with me here. I dunno why I thought she would. I'm so stupid."

"Don't say that. You didn't know."

"Yeah I did but I forced it on her to make myself feel better. Clear my conscious in saying I tried. My presence did nothing but make matters worse."

"You don't know that for sure."

Symone sat up. "Yes I do, Kid. It took her almost two weeks to agree to work with me and the whole time we were training, she fought me every step of the way. If my main intent was *really* about her getting better, I would've paid a physical therapist to work with her."

"What's going on with you, Symone?" Kidera asked concerned. "I've never heard you talk like this."

"She said I tricked her and she's right. I wanted her to get better but—" Symone pointed to herself, "*I* wanted to get better too and I couldn't get my healing without her. I used her illness as a way to serve my own agenda." Symone threw her hands up and leaned back into the loveseat. "I'm selfish."

"Symone—"

"So I'm going back to Charlotte and doing what I should've done from the beginning. I'm gonna give her the space she needs to heal and work through whatever it is she needs to work through. Ant and I are gonna split the cost on a certified physical therapist to work with her three times a week and we're gonna have a nutritionist cook two meals a day for both of them five times a week. Other than that, I have to *truly* trust God to take care of her and even if we never talk again, I have to believe He'll take care of me too."

Kidera did not know what to say. Symone was never one to give up but maybe she was right. Maybe this battle wasn't her fight to begin with. Maybe it was time for her to let go and let God be God.

Kidera was hesitant to ask her next question but she wanted to know. "How are things with you and Regina? I don't mean to pry but after what happened at the family reunion—"

Symone realized she hadn't talked to Kidera since that day. "Wow, naw, we're good. We talked and she was more upset about me being so close with your family and how loving I was with them more than anything but Kyra and Sam were in the wrong in how they handled it, trying to set me up. That was just plain dirty."

"Kyra means well," Kidera defended.

"No, she doesn't. And how she gonna be mad at me for what happened between us when *you* ain't even mad no more?"

Kidera paused for a moment but admitted, "She feels responsible."

"Why?" Symone said with attitude.

"Because she vouched for you."

"What?"

"In high school before we started dating, I asked her about you. I told her you asked me out and that I liked you too but I was afraid of dating an athlete because of all the rumors in y'all being grimy with women. She gave me the green light by vouching for you so she felt she made a bad judgment call after things fell apart."

Symone rolled her eyes. "Great, now I'm a bad judgment call."

"I was just explaining to you why she's acting the way she is."

"And what? She's gonna hold a grudge her whole life?"

"Are you?"

"This is different, Kid. I accept the part I played but it didn't have to go down like that."

"I agree with you. I didn't say you have to forget what happened. She was wrong, I told her that, and I know the friendship between you two will never be the same. But you can forgive and still be cautious to not let it happen again."

"You right. I *can* forgive and be cautious by not having her in my life no more."

"The both of you are stubborn."

"Well, she drew the line and jumped over it. I'm being the bigger one by walking away for good this time." Symone smiled half-heartedly and said, "At least one good thing came from all that drama."

"What's that?"

"I learned how to love Regina better." Symone removed her phone from its holster on her hip and showed Kidera the text messages between she and Regina. "I'm trying to do better at expressing my feelings so I send her little messages throughout the day to let her know I'm thinking about her."

Kidera read a few of the texts but noticed something peculiar. "She hasn't responded back to most of these."

Symone put the phone away and replied, "Yeah, ever since Labor Day, she's been working on a big project at work. Most of the time, she really doesn't have her phone near her. Boss lady makes everybody leave their phones in their office so they can concentrate on work."

"Oh, ok." Kidera still thought it was weird that Regina wouldn't text all day but she left it alone. She was happy that she and Symone were able to reestablish their friendship and not have it interfere with Symone's relationship with Regina.

"Yeah, I still send them so when she gets home she can read them and smile."

"You really do love her."

"I do and I'm trying everything I can think of to make sure she knows it."

Chapter 37

"And I am praying that you will put into
action the generosity that comes from your
faith as you understand and experience all the
good things we have in Christ."
~ Philemon 1:6

"SYMONE," BISHOP REED SAID surprised when he
saw her standing in his doorway, "did we have a meeting
today?"

"No sir. I just stopped by to let you know I was
leaving in the morning."

"You're going back to Charlotte?"

"Yeah, I think it's time."

Bishop Reed sat his pen down and waved Symone
into his office. She was reluctant to enter but she
accepted the invite and sat across from the mahogany
desk.

"You weren't expecting to leave this soon, I
presume," Bishop Reed said.

"I dunno what I was expecting, Bishop. I've been
thinking a lot about what you said about my motives for
being here, that they may've been wrong."

"And?"

"Well, yesterday, the family did a prayer circle and
healing being blocked by unforgiveness was the highlight

of the prayer. Needless to say, my mom didn't receive the message well and she said I tricked her into training her."

"Do you feel like you tricked her?" Bishop Reed asked.

"When you first mentioned it, no. I just figured the reason behind me being here wasn't important as long as my mom got what she needed."

"And what do you think now?"

"I think she would be a lot further along in her recovery if I just would've stayed away."

"That's a tough realization to accept."

"You think?" Symone looked up at Bishop Reed guiltily. "Sorry."

Bishop Reed intertwined his fingers and sat them on his desk. "The question you need to ask yourself is, are you leaving because you feel you failed or because you're finally allowing God to handle it for you?"

Symone thought about the question then responded, "Both." She shifted her weight in the chair and explained, "Because I failed, I'm finally giving it over to God. But—" she stopped Bishop Reed from cutting in, "I've learned if I would've given it to Him from the beginning, I could've saved myself a lot of heartache."

"Can I ask you something, Symone."

"Sure."

"Have *you* forgiven your mother for her negative actions against you?"

"Yes," Symone answered without hesitation.

"Are you sure? Think before you answer, Symone."

"I have forgiven her, Bishop. I mean, it still hurts but—"

"Do not mistake passiveness for forgiveness." Bishop Reed saw Symone had a confused looked on her face so he explained, "You haven't been around your family in years. When you don't have to face that negativity everyday, it's easy to think you've forgiven someone. However, if those feelings of hurt, rage, disappointment, guilt, whatever it may be, if those emotions flood you immediately when you see those people again, those emotions have control over you instead of you having control over the emotions. The distance only played as a buffer but true forgiveness and healing hasn't taken place yet."

"I never looked at it like that."

"You've been thinking these unforgiveness messages are for your mother but it sounds like these messages were meant for you. God is telling you to forgive your mom and your aunts and uncles for the pain they've caused you and once you do that, it will send forth your faith for Him to change their hearts."

"It's so hard though, Bishop," Symone said fighting back tears.

"Symone, if forgiveness was easy no one would struggle with it." Bishop Reed handed Symone a tissue to dry her eyes. "God has blessings in store for you beyond what you could ever imagine. Trust Him at His word, Symone. Do your part and the path will be clear for Him to finish His on your behalf."

Chapter 38

"The LORD says, "I will give you back what you lost to the swarming locusts, the hopping locusts, the stripping locusts, and the cutting locusts." ~ Joel 2:25

"YOU GOT EVERYTHING?"

Symone stood deep in thought with her hands on her hips. "Yep," she finally said.

Antoine grabbed Symone's suitcase and walked toward the front door. Symone snuck up behind Brianna who was watching television.

"I know you're not gonna just sit there and not give me a hug."

Brianna folded her tiny arms across her chest, dropped her head and poked out her bottom lip. "I don't want you to go."

"I don't want to go but my home is somewhere else."

"Why can't you live here?"

"'Cause I gotta go to work but you can come visit me and I'll be back to visit you."

Brianna looked up at Symone with her teary brown eyes and said, "Promise?"

Symone picked Brianna up and kissed her on her cheek. "Promise."

Brianna wrapped her arms around Symone's neck and hugged her before Symone put her down.

Symone walked over to Nicole and gave her a hug.

"Aww, it was great having you here," Nicole said.

"I appreciate you putting up with me."

"Any time and don't be a stranger."

"I won't."

Symone walked outside where Antoine waited with Nathaniel in his arms. Symone kissed Nathaniel on the forehead. "Terrific two's not terrible two's okay lil' man?"

Nathaniel blushed and buried his face in Antoine's neck. Symone smiled at his shyness.

"It's been one crazy summer, huh?" Antoine said.

Symone stuffed her hands into her jacket pocket and grunted solemnly. "You can say that again but everything that happened was needed."

"Growth."

"All day long." Symone gave Antoine half a hug then got into her SUV.

Antoine knocked on the driver side window and said, "Call or text when you get there."

Symone nodded and waved as she pulled out the driveway. She reached for her cell phone and placed it in its holder on the dashboard. Symone started dialing her father's number but ended the call before it went through. Their relationship grew the most during the trip so she thought it was only right to say goodbye to him in person.

Symone walked through the unlocked screen door and found her dad in the living room watching the *Speed* channel.

"Symone," he said, pleasantly surprised to see her.

"Hey dad. I was about to get on the road and thought I'd swing by to see you before I go."

Frederick stood to his feet. "I'm glad you did."
He walked over and hugged Symone.

"You have my number," Symone began, "so
don't be afraid to use it more often."

"I was thinking we could do Thanksgiving dinner
here at the house next month. If you don't have plans
already, you should come by and bring Regina with you.
I'd like to meet her."

"I think she made plans with her family," Symone
replied. "But I'll check and let you know."

"All right. Well, I love you and I'll keep praying
for you."

"I love you, too, dad."

Symone embraced Frederick again but this time,
she felt someone watching them. She opened her eyes
and saw her mother staring at them from the living room
threshold. Symone released her father and walked over to
Paula. She stood in front of her not sure of what to say or
do.

Paula's mouth opened but no words escaped.
Symone gave a half-hearted smile, kissed her on the cheek
and said, "I'll see you, ma."

As Symone headed toward the door, she heard
Paula cry out, "I don't want to die." Symone stopped and
turned to face her. "You asked me," Paula repeated, "I
don't want to die."

The tears poured down Symone's face without
warning. She moved gingerly to Paula's side and sobbed,
"I don't want you to die either." Symone knelt down in
front of her mother and grasped both of her hands. "I'm
sorry. I'm so sorry," she cried over and over.

Paula reached up and cradled Symone's face. Her
soft, frail touch was one Symone hadn't felt in a long time
but craved for everyday of her life. Symone rested her
head in Paula's lap just as she used to do when she was a
little girl. She closed her eyes and allowed herself to be

vulnerable in her mother's arms while her father sung praises of joy behind them.

Part Four

Chapter 39

"Patient endurance is what you need now, so that
you will continue to do God's will. Then you will
receive all that he has promised."
~ Hebrews 10:36

*HI, YOU'VE REACHED REGINA Stewart. Unfortunately
I'm unable to answer the phone but if you leave your name and
number, I will return your call at my earliest convenience. Thank
you and have a blessed day. Beep.*

"Hey Reggie," Symone spoke to the voicemail, "I
wanted to let you know I'm back in North Carolina, less
than thirty miles from the house. You'll never gonna
believe what happened with my mom today. It's too
much to leave on your voicemail but I'll give you a hint.
It's great news! It's finally over, baby. Everything that's
been holding me back is gone. I feel like doors have
opened and now I can finally move forward with you,
basketball and the organization I want to start. But I'm
almost home so I'll tell you all about it when I get there.
I've missed you so much. Can't wait to see you. I love
you, Reggie."
Symone parked her Infiniti QX4 in front of the
house and saw no signs of life. The lights weren't on and
she could see no movement on the inside. Symone got

out the SUV and stretched her body, waking it from its stiff position. She opened the rear hatch, grabbed her luggage and headed to the front door.

Symone dropped her bags just inside the door.

"Reggie!" Symone walked through the living room to the kitchen. "Reggie! You home?"

When there was no answer, Symone called Regina's phone again.

Hi, you've reached...

"Man!" Symone pressed the 'End' button in frustration. *She could still be at work*, Symone thought. *I know, I'll surprise her with dinner.*

Symone went to the refrigerator and found it empty of all perishable items. Milk, eggs, even the turkey sausage was gone.

Symone checked her watch. It was 9:47pm, too late to defrost anything so she opted to order out. She sifted through the coupon drawer until she found an ad for *Maggiano's*. Symone called the number and ordered Regina's favorite dish from the Italian restaurant, Linguine de Mare.

"Tonight, we're celebrating," Symone smiled as she headed down the hall to the bedroom.

The door to the bedroom was closed and it dawned on Symone that Regina may be sleeping. She worked so hard the last month and a half, maybe she came home and tuned out the world for some peace and quiet.

Symone crept up to the door and gently tapped on it before entering. Regina was not there. In fact, the room felt empty except for the beam of light from the street lamp outside that shone through the bedroom window. It casted a spotlight on the perfectly made but empty bed like a stage without a leading lady.

"Reggie?" Symone called faintly.

The hairs on the back of Symone's neck rose in fear as she stepped further into the room. Regina's personal hygiene items were not on the dresser. In their place rested an envelope with Symone's name scribbled across the front in Regina's handwriting.

Confused, Symone leaned against the dresser and opened the envelope. She immediately grew sick to her stomach as she read the enclosed letter.

Symone,
I'm sorry for leaving like this but it was the only way I would've been able to leave. I've tried to tell you this face to face and over the phone but the words never came out. I love you so much and I know you love me too but it hasn't been enough. I want so much more in a relationship, from the person I'm in a relationship with but you haven't been able to give it to me. I've stayed this long because I thought if I was patient, God would place inside you what I needed from you, the emotional and affectionate side of love. Then I saw you with Kidera and her family. I saw everything I ever wanted from you but you shared it with her and her family. I never even knew you had the ability to express love openly but now I know you just don't have it in you to express it to me.
I feel that Kidera still has your heart and it hurts so much because of the 4 years we've shared together but I can't ignored the signs any longer. Kidera still holds the key to unlocking the love inside you and I can't fight for something someone else already possesses. You may think I'm wrong in saying that but if I am wrong, how is it that her and her family were the ones who could 'ignite' (your words not mine) the passion in you to show love? It's time for me to find the one I can ignite. I wished it was you. I prayed it was you but…maybe it just wasn't meant to be. I feel like the rebound girl who lasted way longer than I was

*supposed to. I'm older now and I know what I want
and you continue to show me over again that you can't
give it to me. It's okay, I'm not mad but it's time for
me to be happy. It's time that I'm #1 in someone's
life just as Kidera is #1 in yours.*

Regina

Symone's shoulders slumped forward as she carried her defeated body to the made up bed. She did not need to look in the walk-in closet to see if Regina's clothes were still there. She knew that they were gone, too.

Symone felt each of her pockets until she found her cell phone. She may not know where Regina was but she knew someone who did.

"Hello?"

"Sam, where's Reggie?"

Samantha sighed heavily into the phone. "I can't tell you, Symone."

"Please Sam."

"I promised her I wouldn't."

Symone rubbed her forehead in anguish. "How long she been gone?"

"She moved out a week after getting back in town." *A week?* Symone thought. *How did I not know?*

"Sam, you know I love Regina with everything inside me. I need her here."

With a cynical tone, Samantha snapped, "Regina felt differently."

"Well, she's wrong!" Symone fired back. Her emotions fluctuated back and forth from sadness to anger. "How can she spend one day, one day and be like, Kid still got my heart. Then to tell me in a Dear John letter?"

"Symone—"

"I've been trying, Sam," Symone cried. "I've been trying so hard since she left and she never said a word. She made me believe everything was okay."

"She—she didn't know how to tell you."

"And after four years, she thought this was the best way?"

Samantha remained quiet, not able to defend her best friend's actions.

"I've been trying," Symone repeated. "Does none of that count? Look, can you just tell her to call me?"

"I can't, Symone."

"Please, Sam," Symone pleaded. "Just tell her I wanna talk, no expectations."

Symone could tell by Samantha's deep sigh that she had broken through her exterior walls. "Fine. I'll tell her you want to talk but I can't promise she'll contact you. She's moved on."

"Moved on?" Symone said surprised. Before Symone could ask for clarification, Samantha disconnected the line.

Symone lay back on the bed and stared at the ceiling. *What did Samantha mean when she said Regina moved on? She's only been home six weeks. Was Regina seeing someone else already? How could that be?*

Chapter 40

"So you see, faith by itself isn't enough. Unless it
produces good deeds, it is dead and useless."
~ James 2:17, 22

"THANKS FOR MEETING ME." Symone stood to her
feet as Regina approached the table.

It was the first week of December. Symone was
still adjusting to her new life in Charlotte without Regina.
She didn't call Regina as often as she did when they first
broke up stating in a voice message that she was giving
her the space she needed to figure out what was best for
her. After two months of minimal contact with no
response back, Symone finally received the text she'd
been waiting for. The week before Thanksgiving Regina
texted her stating she was ready to talk. Symone was so
excited she bought a new outfit for the meet.

"You look nice," Regina said as she sat down
across from her.

Symone brushed her hands down the concord red
cardigan sweater and cleared her throat. "So do you."
Symone admired how the fitted jeans and black leather
jacket cuffed Regina's curves. "How you been?"

"I'm okay," Regina said with a nervous smile.

The awkward silence made Symone so nervous
she blurted out the first thing that came to mind. "I've
missed you so much, Reggie."

"Symone—"

"Why didn't you just tell me how you felt, Reggie?" Symone cut in. "Why just up and leave like that?"

"You made me feel like I was worth nothing to you." Regina turned her head to hide the hurt that still lingered.

"But that's not true."

Regina rolled her eyes in discontent.

Symone reached across the table, grabbed her hand and continued, "Okay, okay. What I'm trying to say is—I get what you were saying in your letter. I lost you way before Labor Day, way before I left for Virginia. That stuff with Kid and her family—maybe I never switched y'all places in my heart back then. I didn't know—I didn't see it 'til you brought it up and I'm sorry I put you through that." Regina motioned to speak but Symone raised her hand to quiet her. "I also want to say that I know that most if not all of what happened was my fault. Everything with my mom—"

Regina leaned forward and said, "Your mom having a stroke is not your fault, Symone."

"I know but this thing between us had nothing to do with my mom getting sick." Symone pulled her hands away and scratched her forehead. She straightened her posture and admitted, "I never let you in and for the longest time I convinced myself the reason was because I was trying to protect you but honestly, I was scared. I thought I was too broken for you, with my past being the way it was. I was scared if I let you in you'd figure out I wasn't worth the trouble and that you could do better than me. I was scared you'd leave me."

"Symone—"

"I know it sounds stupid. I didn't even want to admit it to myself because that would be admitting that I have insecurities when it comes to relationships and me protecting you sounded better than me being insecure with what we had." Symone paused to collect her thoughts then continued, "I didn't let you in because I thought you were gonna leave me eventually anyway so I kept you at a distance so when you did leave, it wouldn't hurt as much. I could handle that being the reason why we didn't work but I couldn't handle you telling me you didn't love me anymore and me not knowing why. Kid did that and it ate me up. I couldn't handle reliving that again."

"You've always been so closed off, Symone and I knew that. I knew you had trust issues but that didn't stop me from trying in the beginning. You just—I thought things would get better and then—"

"Yeah, I know."

Symone never regretted anything in her life but at that moment, she wished she never brought Regina to Kidera's family reunion. She unintentionally set into motion the beginning of the end for them.

Symone held back tears as she carried on, "I'm so sorry, baby. I should've done more to show you how much you mean to me."

Regina used the napkin on the table to dab the corner of her eyes. This was the first time Symone ever expressed her feelings for her verbally. "Things happen for a reason, Symone."

"No." Symone shook her head. "Things happen because of the decisions we make, decisions *I've* made." Symone grabbed Regina's hands again and held them tightly in hers. "All I ever wanted was to bring you happiness and I'm at a point now where I feel I can really do that."

"Symone—"

"I've learned a lot about myself Reggie and if you'd just give me another chance, I promise—"

"I'm seeing someone, Symone." Regina blurted out.

Symone stopped suddenly and looked at Regina confused. "Seeing someone? Like, dating?"

"Yes."

"But, wait—" Symone tried to hide how upset she was. "We've only been apart," Symone paused and purposefully counted aloud on her fingers, "October, November, two months. How you meet somebody already?"

Regina hesitated then responded, "It's someone I already knew."

"Who? It's that Zen chick, ain't it?" Regina didn't respond. "I told you!" Symone said through gritted teeth. "I told you she was sitting back, waiting for the right time—"

"Then why didn't you prevent it from happening?" Regina shouted in an accusatory tone. "If you knew, why didn't you do *your* job."

"She stole you from me!"

"No, you let me go and she was there to catch me when I fell."

Regina's words stung Symone to the core but she wasn't giving up. "Well, I want you back."

"It—it doesn't work like that, Symone."

Symone sat back in the chair and shook her head. "It's not going to last, Reggie. She's a rebound. You know that."

"Maybe but—"

"Marry me, Reggie."

Regina stared at Symone in shock. "What?"

"Marry me."

"You don't mean that, Symone. You'd say anything right now to not lose me for good."

"Then why did I come prepared?" Symone reached into her sweater pocket and pulled out a ring box. She slid out of her chair and knelt down on one knee in front of Regina. "I've had this since the night of the draft. I wanted to propose *that* night but things didn't work out the way I planned."

Tears weld up in Regina's eyes. "Symone—"

"I'm so in love with you, Regina Stewart. I know I haven't let you in all the way but I want to. I'm ready to trust myself to be vulnerable with you. I've known for a long time that I wanted to spend the rest of my life with you but this time apart proved it even more. I'm lost without you, Reggie. So, I'll ask you again." Symone opened the ring box and revealed a 1 ½ ct diamond ring in a vintage style frame made from 24K two-tone gold. "Will you marry me?"

Regina's eyes bounced back and forth between Symone and the ring. "Symone, I—" Regina closed her eyes and the tears trickled down her cheeks. "I—I can't."

"Why not?"

"We're not there. I don't know if we ever were."

Symone stared at Regina surprised. She closed the ring box and slid back into her seat. "So, this is it? You just—"

"I'm sorry, Symone," Regina cried. "I just can't anymore."

Before Symone could say or do anything to stop her, Regina stood up and rushed out the deli.

Back to Present Day:
Memorial Day
Weekend 2012

Post-game Analysis

SYMONE SMILED AS KAYLEIGH slinked back to Regina's side.

"I can get you guys season tickets," Symone offered.

"That's okay, we already have some."

"Oh ok, well—"

"There are my girls—whoa!" Symone stood and watched as an older woman in her late thirties smiled at her with dancing eyes. "Symone Holmes! I can't believe it. I'm such a huge fan of yours."

"Uh thanks." Symone was irritated the woman interrupted the conversation between her and Regina but she remained polite as the woman rambled on, "I've been a fan since you days in Houston. When I heard the Dream picked you up, I knew we'd become regulars at the games."

"We?" Symone asked confused. She didn't see anyone else with the woman.

"You didn't tell her, Reggie?"

Symone coughed violently at the sound of the woman calling Regina by the same pet name she used to call her.

The woman rushed over and patted Symone on the back. "You okay?"

"Yeah."

"Toni, do you mind going to get the car?" Regina asked.

"Sure baby."

"And take Kayleigh with you please." Kayleigh waved bye to Symone as Toni bent down to pick her up. Toni looked at Kayleigh and saw that Symone had autographed her jersey. Toni began thanking her but Symone was lost in a daze.

"Toni, please," Regina pleaded.

"Right." Toni leaned into Regina and whispered not quite low enough, "Ask her over to dinner," before she skipped off toward the parking lot.

"You let her call you Reggie?" Symone finally said when Toni and Kayleigh were out of earshot.

"I—"

"That's my name for you!"

"Symone—"

"Naw, Reggie—" Symone rolled her eyes and exhaled loudly in frustration, "now it don't sound right coming out my mouth after hearing her say it."

"Will you listen?"

Symone didn't even hear Regina's plea. "I mean, I know that's probably your girl and all and I respect that but some things should stay sacred, ya know. And what's up with her Kango? She do know it's 2012, not 1998, right? Upgrade your girl to a Fedora and tell her to untuck her sweater from her pants, looking like—"

"Symone!"

"What?"

"She's my wife," Regina said folding her arms across her chest.

Symone stumbled a few steps backward as if someone kicked her in the stomach. She assumed Regina and Toni were a couple but married? Her mind struggled to process the information.

Symone recovered her speech but "So—married, huh?" was all she managed to say.

"Yes, almost 5 years now in Hawaii."

"Hawaii?"

"You know I always wanted to get married or have my honeymoon in Hawaii."

"Yeah, I know. It was *our* plan, remember?"

Regina swallowed hard but refused to answer.

Symone thought about Kayleigh and remembered she was five years old. "So Kayleigh's—"

"Yes, we planned her together."

"Wow." Symone was speechless. She had so many questions but she wasn't sure if she wanted to know the answers to any of them. "So, I'm guessing Toni doesn't know about our history then, huh?"

Regina relaxed her posture but kept her arms crossed. "She knows we went to college together. She's seen the softball team photos but," Regina shook her head, "no, I didn't tell her we were in a relationship. I found out the hard way that having a pro athlete as an ex brings out the insecurities in others."

"I guess. So, what ever happened to Zen?"

"She was the first to display those insecurities," Regina said. "I tried to stay in touch with you—"

"Yeah, I know." Symone cleared her throat. "I just—it was hard for me to see you with someone else. All I could think about was sabotaging the relationship and I knew that wasn't gonna help me get you back."

"I'm glad you realized that."

"I tried to keep tabs on *you* through Sam once I left Charlotte but Kyra got on her for talking to me so—"

"I know. Sam told me."

Symone looked at Regina and smiled weakly. "I guess I should've expected that since ya'll best friends and all."

"They're married now."

"Kids?"

"They adopted a little boy a few years ago."

"That's cool."

Regina rocked side to side, trying to think of something else to say beside the obvious. "Now that we're living in the same city again, you should come by the house and visit sometime."

"Naw, I don't think I can do that," Symone said. "Don't get me wrong, I'm happy for you and all but Toni's living the life I was supposed to have with you. I can't see that up close and personal."

"At least stay in touch, this time. Kayleigh would be happy to find out her mom is friends with her favorite player."

"Friends," Symone repeated with a touch of sadness. "I guess that's where we are now."

Regina opened her mouth to respond but she changed her mind. The only response she had was one of agreement and she knew she didn't need to say it for Symone to accept its truth.

"Can I ask you a question?" Symone's brow furrowed as she tried to think of the plainest way to ask, "When exactly did you stop loving me? Was there anything I could've done to change things?"

Before Regina could answer, Toni pulled up to the curb and honked the horn. She waved emphatically. "It was awesome meeting you, Symone!" she shouted with a bright grin.

Symone threw a quick but face smile in her direction.

Regina took a step toward the car but turned around. She walked over and gave Symone a big hug. Symone closed her eyes and inhaled the familiar aroma of *Hypnose* perfume.

She's still wearing my favorite scent, Symone thought.

As Regina pulled away, she whispered, "I never stopped loving you, Symone. There's nothing you could do to ever—" Regina purposely choked on her words to prevent them from reigniting a fire that took her years to extinguish.

Symone's heart skipped a beat right before it dropped to the pit of her stomach. She watched in agony as Regina hurried to the car, hopped into the passenger side seat and rode off with her family.